The Tree and the Vine

The Tree and the Vine

DOLA DE JONG

Afterword by Lillian Faderman
Translated by Ilona Kinzer

The Feminist Press
at The City University of New York
New York

© 1955, 1961 by Dola de Jong
Afterword © 1996 by Lillian Faderman
All rights reserved.

Published 1996 by The Feminist Press at The City University of
New York, 311 East 94 Street, New York, New York 10128-5684,
by arrangement with Feministische Uitgeverij VITA, Amsterdam.

99 98 97 96   4 3 2 1

Library of Congress Cataloging-in-Publication Data
De Jong, Dola, 1911-
    The tree and the vine / by Dola de Jong ; afterword by Lillian
Faderman.
        p. cm.
    ISBN 1-55861-140-1. — ISBN 1-55861-141-X (alk. paper)
    1. Netherlands—History—German occupation, 1940-1945—
Fiction. 2. Jewish women—Netherlands—Fiction. 3. Lesbians—
Netherlands—Fiction. I. Title.
PS3507.E395T74 1996
839.3' 1362—dc20   95-38608
                                    CIP

Printed in the United States of America with soy-based ink on
acid-free paper by McNaughton & Gunn, Inc.

This publication is made possible, in part, by public funds from the
National Endowment for the Arts and the New York State Council
on the Arts. The Feminist Press is also grateful for a grant from the
John D. and Catherine T. MacArthur Foundation. The Feminist
Press would like to thank Joanne Markell and Genevieve Vaughan
for their generosity.

Chapter One

I MET Erica in 1938 at the house of Wies, a mutual friend. On my side, I considered Wies no more than a superficial acquaintance, a woman I saw occasionally to preserve the amenities. For six weeks we had occupied adjoining beds in a hospital ward. This had not inspired me with a desire to know her any better and at the end of the month and a half I had had my fill of her. Wies is one of those women who, whenever she encounters a member of the same sex, spreads out and tightens a net of women's solidarity, and she possesses the thickness of skin characteristic of her kind. My lack of response did not affect her and if I pretended sleepiness it only seemed to encourage her to more confidential revelations.

To escape her by flight was denied me in the hospital. Even though she left two weeks earlier than I, she kept me in her debt by return visits with flowers and delicacies. After my recovery I did not feel I could ignore her altogether and occasionally accepted one of her frequent invitations. My unwillingness to offend people was at least partially my excuse. This was a weakness I still had when I met Erica.

One hot summer night, then, I had gone to visit Wies. I confess I hoped she would not be home. Then I could leave a note and would have done my duty. But when I rang the bell the door opened, and I was trapped again.

Erica was lying on a couch near the open balcony doors. When we were introduced she seemed to hesitate for a moment between rising and staying where she was. My outstretched hand decided her; swinging her legs easily from the couch, she rose. I felt immediately attracted to her, forgetting the less pleasant aspects of my visit. Now, after all these years, I can still see Erica as she slid from that couch and took my hand. She had a young full face, but there were tired lines about her mouth which pulled it down at the corners. Her brown eyes had a penetrating, somewhat melancholy expression. She was wearing sandals, navy blue woollen socks, a pleated skirt, and a red sports blouse open at the throat. Her blonde hair was cut short with an untidy fringe at the neck, like a boy who badly needs a haircut. She was dressed more or less like a member of the socialist youth organization—a particular type with which I had never felt at ease. We had a few girls like that working at the office and I always kept away from them. But Erica seemed different. That first evening she gave me the impression that she adopted this schoolgirl attire because she couldn't quite accept the responsibility of being grown up. It occurred to me later that maybe she couldn't afford anything better. I no longer attach any value to that theory either.

That evening at Wies'—a chance encounter—Erica's life became part of mine. I have often asked myself since what my life would have been like without Erica. For a long time afterward I continued to think my role was only that of a spectator. Now I know that I changed the course of my life because of her. Whether it was better that way, or whether I would have been happier without her, who can tell? I am certainly the last to know.

One month after our meeting, we were living together. I had been wanting to move for a long time; I had had enough of landladies and of the boarding-school routine of the women's residence where I had lived, mainly through inertia, since the death of my father. Erica was looking for a place of her own after a final decisive quarrel with her mother.

The lease of the apartment on the Prinsengracht, one of those old streets along a canal, was in my name. Erica was working as a journalist for the *Nieuwe Post* and was earning the salary of a beginner. She was one step above the level of "voluntary worker"—a title which was held out as bait in those days to exploit the young. For two years she had worked as a "volunteer" for a provincial paper and had lived on her mother's income. Now she was paying "Ma" back: a kind of vicious circle by which many young people were victimized in those days of depression.

The way Erica spoke of her mother that first year made me laugh. Whatever happened, she stressed only the humour in it. At the time I did not understand what was behind all this joking, and merely relished Erica's descriptive talent when she talked about Ma.

"Ma phoned," she would call, climbing our stairs after a day at the office. "The General is taking a holiday but Ma can't go along!" And upstairs she would give a colourful report of her mother's complaints about the retired war-horse for whom she kept house.

That first year with Erica on the Prinsengracht was full of surprises. Now I can hardly imagine why I accepted her often strange behaviour with so little resistance or comment. Of course I was aware of her troubles and conflicts, but in those days they were projected like silhouettes on a white screen. Only later did these images assume shape and colour through the perspective of their background. The torture of insight and understanding was spared me during that year simply because I tried to stay aloof.

We had decided to live our separate lives. That was the arrangement we had made from the beginning, an arrangement prompted by a childlike desire to preserve a certain imagined freedom. We did not make a point of it, of course;

it was somehow lodged in our minds as an idea needing no justification. It was simply a reaction to our younger days when we were rarely provided—though Erica probably somewhat more than I—with the opportunity to express our urge for freedom. As I see it now, we clung to that condition desperately. It prevented me from giving and accepting a deeper friendship. The effort to avoid mixing in one another's lives made that first year together a *tour de force*, and for me a long exercise in self-discipline.

Because of Erica's unpredictable nature, there was no regularity whatever in our household. Yet we did establish a certain routine to which we could keep without difficulty. We wasted no discussion on it; our life developed without plan.

I had persuaded the landlord to tear down a wall, which added the middle room to Erica's quarters. My bed stood against the sliding doors. Although those doors were always shut we could talk together at night before going to sleep, since our voices carried easily from her bed in the alcove to mine by the doors.

Those doors between our rooms I had closed even before I signed the lease. We had come for the third time to look over the apartment, to be quite sure we had made the right choice. The renting of an apartment, and the responsibilities connected with it, caused me a certain anxiety which I felt especially at night when I was alone. Before Erica I concealed it. That Sunday afternoon I was standing in the back room while Erica was in the middle room.

"Are you sure you want the front room, Erica?"

She nodded with conviction. "Yes, I'd rather have the noise of cars and such, you know, the street noises, than *that*." She pointed to the open balcony doors which looked out on the backs of houses on the street parallel to the Prinsengracht. "Fishwives and family quarrels!" she added.

"I've had enough of that!" I did not understand what she meant, since the General's house where Erica had been living with her mother was on the residential It Straat. But I let it pass.

"We'll have that wall torn down so you'll get the middle room. Otherwise you don't get your share; my room is much bigger. There is enough space for your bed, and perhaps a small table..."

"...Have the wall torn down?" she repeated after me. "Do you think the landlord is crazy?"

"Just leave it to me," I said, suddenly very sure of myself. "If we have to, we'll pay for it ourselves."

She gave me a searching look. "You know I haven't any money. But if you're so sure of the landlord..."

"All right," I said, "shall we sign?"

She nodded slowly, without enthusiasm, without taking her eyes from me. First I closed the balcony doors, as if to postpone the final action, and then with a look of understanding to Erica—to which she did not react—I closed the sliding doors. This gesture was meant to put a seal on our agreement to leave each other free. At that moment I could not express it in words.

Our decision, which we afterward celebrated with a cup of coffee in a cafeteria, was only an epilogue. Erica was taciturn; we emptied our cups and went our own ways. The next morning she phoned me from her office.

"When are you going to sign?"

"During lunch hour."

"Don't forget about that wall!"

In the weeks that followed, Erica was enthusiastic—she ignored with a stubborn optimism the little obstacles that always come with settling down in a new apartment. She left it to me to overcome them all. The consent of the landlord to

tear down the wall had apparently convinced her of my skill
in such matters. I did not tell her that I had had to sign a two-
year lease in order to get his cooperation. "You settle that,"
she said invariably when I brought up subjects like wallpaper,
floor covering, and heating. Encouraged by her confidence, I
went ahead with several alterations I would never have risked
under different circumstances. I even went into debt for her.
Erica was completely absorbed with the furnishing of her
room. She was incredibly handy with tools. I had never seen a
woman who could do carpentry as well as she. Her short firm
fingers handled wood and hammer with astounding ease.

She had no money for furniture or any other household
goods, but she dragged all sorts of cast-off objects home to
the Prinsengracht and at night she hammered and worked
away until she had the beginnings of a primitively furnished
room. When I returned to my rooming house around midnight—I used to go to the Prinsengracht in the evenings
then, like a cat which wants to familiarize itself with new
surroundings—the light in her room would still be burning.
I would leave Erica behind, bent over that night's project,
one knee holding a piece of wood in place, the saw in her
firm hand, her straight hair hanging over her eyes, the sports
blouse dark with perspiration. The rasping of the saw or the
blows of the hammer would follow me a long way down the
street. The next evening, when I asked her whether she had
worked very late, she would answer casually, "Till about four,
I guess; it was getting light. It is very quiet here at night—
at least I know that." Or, "I stayed here all night; it wasn't
worth going home any more." And she would point to a
chair she had just upholstered. "Try it. See how comfortable
it is." She was used to being up at all hours. I kept asking
myself whether she would keep me awake at night. I needed
eight hours of undisturbed sleep.

Unexpectedly, she took over the moving of my bed and other belongings. My suggestion to call a mover was immediately rejected with "That's a waste of money."

"But what else?" I asked hesitatingly, intimidated by the tone of her voice, which made my idea sound suddenly so extravagant.

"We'll see."

She left me in suspense until the last day and finally when I timidly reminded her of it, she said, "Pa's warehouse man is coming with a pushcart tomorrow afternoon at five-thirty. See that everything's ready." It was the first time I had heard her mention Pa. Until then I had assumed that her father was dead, and that Ma, being a widow, was forced to earn her own living. That was the logical conclusion I had drawn from her silence on the matter, but apparently it was wrong. Even then she added nothing to her statement and I hadn't the courage to pursue the subject.

I remember vividly the first evening in our new apartment. The warehouseman had had to make the trip between my room and the apartment twice. The first time his pushcart was already half-filled with Erica's stuff that he had picked up at the General's house. When he finally left with "regards to Pa" from Erica and a five-guilder tip from me, we turned to the chaos inside. Until eleven o'clock we were busy arranging our possessions. We lost a lot of time walking back and forth through the hall, for even then the sliding doors between our rooms remained closed. It was only after we returned from a snack in a restaurant nearby, and after I had inspected the result of Erica's activities, that I suddenly knew what had bothered me vaguely all during the moving. I had missed something, but in the commotion and confusion I had not realized what it was. Her things on the pushcart—some boxes, a suitcase, a chair, a typewriter—had

evoked a brief feeling of pity in me, but the thought of her
"new" furniture already in the apartment reassured me. Her
room did strike me as rather bare, but I attributed that to the
moving, and thought it was merely a question of unpacking
and arranging. But when we said goodnight, with Erica
standing in a corner of her room untying a rope around a
roll of blankets, I knew.

"Erica, your bed! Where is your bed? You've forgotten
your bed!"

She straightened up and looked at me, an embarrassed
smile distorting her mouth. "I sleep on the floor," she said.
In spite of the smile, her voice was serious and decisive.

I insisted, "But you can't! What nonsense..."

"I can sleep anywhere," she interrupted. "I'll buy one
secondhand before long. Don't worry about it."

This last reassurance was apparently because of the
expression on my face: self-reproach for my thoughtlessness,
an unreasoning feeling of indignation.

"Why didn't you tell me? I could have lent you the
money."

She sat down on top of the blanket roll and folded her
arms around her knees. She was laughing aloud now.
"Haven't you ever slept on the floor? What if there were a
fire, or a flood, and you had to?"

"Erica, stop it!" I didn't know what to say. It was just
impossible for me to take the matter lightly; I could not laugh
with her. But she stopped laughing herself. She averted her
head and looked out the window for a few minutes. It was
suddenly so quiet I could hear my clock ticking behind the
doors in my room.

"Ma didn't want to give me the bed," she said finally.
She kept looking out the window at the dark silhouettes of
the trees on the moonlit canal.

"I suppose the bed belonged to the General?" I ventured—a feeble joke to help her which I remember well. That whole episode has always remained unpleasantly clear in my mind.

Erica shrugged her shoulders.

"Well," I said, "sleep well."

"You too."

"Our first night..." What could I say?

"Yes."

I lay awake for hours. It was quiet in the old house on the canal, but sleep would not come.

Erica slept on the floor every night for at least six weeks, wrapped in her blanket like a cocoon. I gave her a bed for her birthday in October. I had not touched on the subject again. Erica's attitude made it impossible. Often the words that would have begun a discussion lay on my tongue, but I could not utter them. Lying in my own bed before going to sleep, or at the office, or on the way home, my silence seemed ridiculous to me. But when I confronted her it was not possible to ask casually, "About that bed—shall we go and have a look tomorrow?" Several times I stood in front of a furniture store window; once I had even gone inside to ask prices and left the salesman with some excuse. When, on that October morning, the bed was delivered very early—the whole thing with all its mysterious arrangements had worried me endlessly—Erica only mumbled "Thank you." But then suddenly she dropped on the bed, bounced up and down, and said, "Just right. Not too soft!"

On that birthday I met Ma. Erica had announced the visit without comment, without jokes. When the bell rang and Erica pulled the front door open, the stairway was suddenly full of sound, exclamations alternated with laughter, exaggerated panting and loud sighs—really as if a solid

column of noise were steadily rising. Then, as Ma arrived at
the top, a calmer version of the same:

"Goodness what a climb, dearie! You are certainly in the
clouds here. Hello child!" (There was a loud kiss.) "Con-
gratulations. I must say, you have a nice place. What you
need is a carpet on those stairs. I'll see to that! Where is
your friend? Dear me! Well, many happy returns! Here—
this is for you."

I was in the kitchen making tea, and waited in vain
for the sound of Erica's voice. Without a word she led her
mother to her room and closed the door. And I stood hesitantly in the hall, tray in hand, not knowing what to do.

A little later I was seated opposite Erica's mother, a big-
boned woman with Erica's mouth, and hair dyed pitch-
black as shoe-polish. It was I who kept the conversation
going—which, I must admit, was no trouble at all. I thought
Ma, as I called her from the start, was fascinating and amusing, full of stories, and with an eager reaction to simple
questions or to any evidence of interest. Erica was taciturn,
as usual.

I had taken the closing of her door—which, after a
moment's hesitation, I had ignored—as a sign she was
ashamed of her mother. Again I was mistaken. She even
smiled at Ma's loud coarse humour; her eyes met mine
without a trace of embarrassment.

Even the spiteful and derisive remarks about "your Pa"
seemed to make no impression. Erica was sitting on the floor
with her arms around her knees, her favourite position,
smoking quietly. I must confess that sometimes I felt embarrassed myself. Whenever a laugh was too boisterous, a story
too improbable, a confession too frank, I involuntarily
sought Erica's eyes to see whether she shared my reaction,
but she remained impassive. It doesn't affect her, I thought

with amazement; she is objective, amused, not even bored with all these stories and jokes she must have heard hundreds of times.

After the departure of Ma, who was dining out with her Colonel—General was purely Erica's title—I went to the kitchen to prepare a festive birthday dinner. But Erica held me back. She had five guilders in her hand.

"Present from Ma," she said. "Let's celebrate."

We dined at Kempinsky's, but Erica ate hardly anything. I had to help pay the bill. After we had emptied two bottles of wine she kept ordering gin. With great difficulty I finally persuaded her to come home. I had to help her undress. She leaned against me sleepily, telling me I was a sweet little bitch, and she kissed me on the neck. Yet on the way home she had talked quite rationally, almost in monologue, speaking with gusto and often with wit about her work at the newspaper and describing her colleagues.

That night I lay awake thinking about the five guilders. "Here—this is for you!" This was the present which coarse fingers had taken out of a dusty little handbag, which was carried upstairs in that noisy ascent to be delivered on the top step. I did not know whom to pity more, the mother or the daughter. Memories of my birthdays at home, the yellow daisies that decorated my place, my fork and knife at the breakfast table, the tastefully wrapped presents around my plate, the birthday cake with candles (lately one for every five years!), my father's silent pleasure...all those things kept coming back.

At breakfast Erica joked about the bed.

"Now I have a bed and I can't sleep."

"What about that gin?" I asked.

"Yes, what about that? I was pretty tight, wasn't I?"

"Slightly."

She shook her head. "You see, then it *was* the bed. And do you know what I thought of?" She looked at me with a comic despair, behind which I felt an effort to make up for something. "Now you will have to get me sheets and pillowcases."

"A nice Christmas present," I said, a bit shy in this role of benefactor.

"Not necessary. I got ten guilders from Pa. You'd better buy them. I don't know anything about things like that."

Before we went to work she gave me the money. "What a waste!" she said. And at the bottom of the stairs she turned and called to me, "Bea...I was supposed to buy a dress with it!" She seemed to think it was funny. She went out laughing.

Thus, in the beginning, I was continually confronted with riddles. But now and then Erica felt like talking. For no reason at all she would start to tell me about her childhood and adolescence, and those conversations helped ease the concern that was always in my mind.

What she said was always depressing or tragic, but at that time I had the impression she didn't see it that way, and usually I laughed at her stories. On such occasions I really didn't get enough sleep. From her past came certain expressions which we used at the appropriate time and which strengthened our sense of intimacy and oneness. We would repeat Pa's complaint to Ma: "One day you'll dance on my grave!" Or: "We're going to Granny's!"—Ma's words when, from the upstairs window, she saw Pa disappearing in a bar opposite.

There came a time when Erica could no longer see the humour of it, but that was much later.

Chapter Two

WIES received the news of our partnership with enthusiasm. She assumed the role of *deus ex machina* and made a great fuss about it. To her mind we were two lonely wanderers, who, after an appeal to her infallible instinct for people, had found solace in each other. It did not enter her mind that providence had played a greater part; after all, my visit to her that summer night was impromptu. But I did not begrudge her the satisfaction. Naturally, although somewhat hesitantly, I revealed to Erica my feeling—or rather, lack of feeling—for Wies. "But," I concluded, "I suppose I'll have to go and see her sometime."

"Why should you?" she asked.

"She means well, and when I was ill she was so nice to me."

"So what? Anyway she did it mostly to please herself. People like Wies are thoughtful and kind for their own gratification."

With these words she had not only outlined Wies' character, but, a relief to my own rather guilty conscience, also thrown light on my visits to Wies. Why she went to see Wies herself now and then I did not know and did not ask. She had told me only that Wies used to work in the newspaper's morgue. But I was sure that, for some reason, she liked Wies. Erica was not one to keep a friendship going in order to please, or out of a need to be liked. She didn't mind making enemies. I could not tell what sort of people she liked, at least not for that first year. In those days I did not see many people, and had few visitors. I avoided certain friends because the loss of my father made me sensitive to certain encounters which would be inevitably painful. The people to whom I introduced Erica she treated with a friendly reserve. Only after about six months—I don't remember exactly how long—did she begin speaking her mind about my friends. In most cases, she was unreasoningly violent in her criticism. I was surprised at that, for by then I knew her essentially tolerant nature and her hidden warmth.

Prompted by curiosity, I went with her once to visit Wies. I wanted to find out what attracted her to that dependent creature who left me so indifferent and irritated, and whom I had been too weak to shake off. When I said I was going with her, Erica raised her eyebrows in surprise, but immediately afterward she said, "How nice." She put her arm in mine, and at her insistence we walked all the way to the south side of the city. She wanted to enjoy the autumn evening. We spoke little. I was tired after a busy day at the office. Erica, who doubtless had a feverish day at the newspaper behind her, evidently wasn't. She just happened to be quiet by nature.

When we passed the Café Parkzicht, she told me that her boss at the paper spent every night there at his special table. Then suddenly and with a frightening excitement, she pulled me across the street right in front of the windows of the café, and commanded me to glance—quickly and above all not obtrusively—inside.

"Look—there on the left—you can see him sitting by the window. Tall and blond with glasses."

I saw nothing and protested loudly. With the same uncontrolled excitement she pushed me back to the other side of the street, to the main entrance of the park. As we crossed the street she kept looking behind her, not at all unobtrusively. She was suddenly behaving like a teenager. I was totally taken aback. She had never made any special mention of her boss; she talked rather less about him than about her other colleagues. Yes, that was the evening I recalled later, when I tried to reconstruct past events in order to put the jigsaw puzzle together.

"We are going through the park, aren't we?" she asked needlessly, and I said, "Yes, of course," and added how lovely it smelled of wet, rotting autumn leaves and that it reminded me of my childhood in The Hague when I cycled home from school past the woods. But the incident stayed in my mind for a long time afterward.

I was aware that Erica didn't like to talk about men. That evening's excited behaviour did not fit in with her nature. But what did she talk about with Wies, whose conversation turned always to men, as I knew from the weeks in the hospital? As far as I was concerned, that was my main count against Wies, and one of the things I appreciated in Erica.

We were walking slowly now, and there were other people like us who said goodbye to the summer that night in the park and tried to content themselves with autumn. I asked myself whether this was not the best season after all, the season of decay and decomposition, which carries in itself the promise of new bloom. Autumn, when it forced itself on me so strongly as it did then, always made me sentimental—even melancholy. Those daily bicycle trips home from school to where my father waited for me with tea had made me that way.

I could not say much, yet I wanted to help Erica with small talk. I thought she must feel that she had behaved peculiarly, though she gave no sign of embarrassment. We walked leisurely through the park to the exit. Slowly the leaves fell from the tired trees, and in the withered carpet our feet played, more discreetly now, the game of our childhood years.

At Wies', Erica immediately threw herself on the couch. She propped a pillow under her head and lay there, completely at home, just as I had found her the first time. Wies was enormously happy. She did her best to please us, and in the process created an atmosphere of uneasiness that made me sit on the edge of my chair. (Yes, Wies, I'm fine here and tea is all right with me and I really don't want anything else and I am not too hot and there is no draught here and I'd really rather sit in this chair than in that one.) Erica was watching it all quietly and did not take her eyes off Wies.

"What do you think of my dress, Erica?" Wies asked her. I noted irritably that the girl who wore a sports blouse and woollen socks, whom I had never heard uttering a serious word about clothes or fashion, said the dress was "darling" and so nice with that Chinese collar, and asked whether Wies was wearing her hair differently. Did she have a permanent, and what had she paid for it? The conversation that evening went beyond all limits, I thought. Stupid gossip about clothes, men, the stubborn cleaning woman who worked for Wies, and about Huib, the ex-husband, whom I knew from stories in the hospital as intimately as if I had seen him turn around in front of the mirror every night in his underwear.

I was irritated, and at the same time annoyed at my own irritation, for, I thought, there was really no reason for any deeper or more interesting conversation. Though I did my best to adjust, I could not take part and I felt stiff and unpleasantly reserved. I reproached myself for a snob. We took a tramcar home and talked about our plans for the next day, Sunday. Erica was completely herself again. We were going to take the train to the beach and walk through the dunes. But that Sunday Erica stayed in bed. She pleaded fatigue and asked to be left alone; I should go my own way and not bother about her.

After that she did this repeatedly. She would sleep the whole Sunday. When I stayed home, I would hear her a few times a day clattering about in the kitchen or in the shower, but otherwise it was stone-still. During the week she got little sleep. Often she would read in bed until far into the night, or she would write. What she wrote, or to whom, I did not know. My vague worry, before the moving, that she would keep me from my sleep, had been pointless. She was quiet as a mouse, and I only knew about her being awake at night because of the sliver of light I saw between the sliding doors when I woke now and then myself. So I could understand that once in a while she would sleep an entire Sunday, and the consistency and logic of it struck me. I too was always as quiet as possible, though Erica never asked it of me.

That first year, then, I was only amused by her days of complete rest; later I began to see a special significance in them and could tell in advance when Erica was going to disappear for an entire Sunday under the blankets.

Thus I hoped repeatedly to have the final insight, but looking back on it again later, I would smile contemptuously—and also a little sadly—because of what I had so flatly called "insight." And even now, with the complete panorama of this human life within my vision, I sometimes wonder whether what I took at a distance for a growing tree was perhaps after all only a lifeless trunk, its own greenery stifled by the vines that grew around it.

Just before Christmas that year Erica inherited three thousand guilders, or rather Ma received it as a legacy from a childless uncle and gave it all to Erica. She had visited her at the newspaper and put the envelope with the money in her hand. When I heard Erica coming upstairs, I knew immediately that something special had happened. She was singing one of those vulgar Dutch ditties; she had a whole repertoire of them and to my great delight she always knew all the words. Whether the song had two verses or ten, Erica remembered them all. On her lips they were doubly entertaining. As she climbed the stairs, she rapped the envelope against the wall, click-clack, click-clack, singing, "To hell with going home..."—the refrain of a well-known drinking song. I knew immediately that she had been drinking. She threw the envelope at me, sank down on a kitchen chair, and, with her head on the table, began laughing softly.

"Ma, the benefactor!" she said at last, wiping tears from her eyes. "Three thousand guilders for Erica!"

What Ma had said, I did not get to know. Erica left the kitchen with the envelope like a rag between her thumb and forefinger, and I drained the potatoes. My heart was pounding, and I had not been able to say a word. After a few moments I became conscious of the frozen smile on my face.

Erica didn't come in to dinner until I was peeling the apple that was my dessert. She piled a fair portion of sauerkraut on her plate and ate with gusto. Now and then I saw her almost imperceptibly shake her head and suppress a new fit of laughter. I peeled a tangerine for her and put the slices carefully along the edge of her plate. As I did so, she suddenly looked full at me, tears welling in her eyes. "Bea, Bea," she said, and then used Grandma's expression: "It's all in a lifetime."

"Let's go to the movies," she went on lightly, as if nothing had happened. "Or why not the theatre? I'm rich now. What time is it? We can just make it."

The race to wash and dress in time was a true relief to me. We saw an American comedy and had coffee in the intermission. On the way home Erica suddenly pulled her arm away from mine. "I'm going for a walk," she said, and turned into a side street. She did not come home until morning.

The money melted away like snow in the sun. We had a
Christmas tree and an English Christmas with presents—a
wrist watch and a new radio for me. Erica bought expensive
dresses and shoes she never wore, piles of books, a record
player and more records than we had room for. Quartets
or piano concertos, Greta Keller or the *Three Penny Opera*
sounded through our floor the whole evening. There were
always wine and gin in the house. At Erica's insistence we
ate in restaurants, went to concerts and did not miss a new
play. She lived in a mad haste to spend the money. At first I
resisted a luxuriousness to which I could not contribute
from my own means, but soon I let myself be treated without protest. The money had better get out of the house as
soon as possible, I thought. If that was her goal, I would not
resist. No criticism—in God's name no criticism! That was a
passion of mine in those days. Live together, all right, but no
censure. If only it would end soon. I could not bear the
feverish atmosphere, the artificial gaiety.

On New Year's Eve the house was suddenly full of people.
Colleagues of Erica's came stomping up the stairs. Young
men with an air of importance behind which they hid a lack
of self-confidence limited themselves to measured phrases
with an affected accent and raised eyebrows. "Really...is that
so?"—or a friendly "Oh, I had no idea!" Aged bachelors, a
little bent from the long disillusion of journalism and the
endless race for the last paragraph, spoke about everything
with protective condescension: "Yes, yes, little girl, that's
how time flies!"—and they proved extremely helpful in
preparing the cold supper. I counted two couples, one quietly amused at us young girls and our apartment, the other
a loud old gentleman who had obviously escaped some bor-
ing family get-together, and his unwilling spouse, wearing
an enormous cameo on her blouse and a necklace of ivory

beads that hung down to her waist, who after her second
glass of hot wine started complaining about the sad fate of a
newspaper man's wife. And there was a nice girl, secretary
to the boss, who as the evening progressed was commis-
sioned to convey frank messages to her employer. I had not
invited anybody; it was Erica's evening, and besides I felt no
need to see my friends in those days.

"And now I'm going to give a party!" Erica had
announced two evenings before. It was a mystery to me how
she had found all these people ready to come at the last
moment, but after the festivities had gone on for about fif-
teen minutes and I had talked to all the guests, I realized
she was providing the loneliest and least popular with a
chance to celebrate the passing of the Old Year. It was the
kind of evening about which you ask yourself, amid full ashtrays and sticky glasses after it is finished, what the sense of
such an enterprise could be—why you started it in the first
place. A feeling of depression comes over you, as if you
hadn't lived up to expectations.

The guests tried right and left to find points of contact,
and when they failed, when the conversations they did start
didn't bring satisfaction, they circulated through the apartment, from Erica's room to mine, then leaned against the
kitchen table and tried to talk to me as I looked after the
refreshments there. It was the kind of party where the most
commonplace stupidities are flung into space with bravura
in order to attract attention, and through that perhaps to
counteract a sense of emptiness. Or where profound obser-
vations remain hanging in a vacuum, like balloons escaped
from a child's hand, slowly disintegrating against the ceiling.

In the beginning Erica did not quite know what to do
with this situation she had created. I understood her rather
timid smile, the incessant smoking, and the aimless moving

from one group to another, and they spurred my effort to put everybody at ease. I did not leave a glass unfilled, brought in the sandwiches and meat-rolls a full hour before I had intended, and talked without stopping. Toward midnight, however, Erica had drunk so much that she was no longer aware of the artificial atmosphere and the scarcely hidden boredom. I am sure that she considered the evening a success, and her toast to the New Year was long and outspoken. Around two o'clock, when the bottom of the punchbowl was visible, my endurance had worn thin; I prayed in silence that someone would stand up, and thus make the others conscious of the late hour.

There was a ring at the doorbell. "Who is that? Who is that?" everybody asked at once. "More visitors!" One of the younger visitors called out, "The more the merrier!"

Erica went to open the door and, suddenly sober and pale with excitement, brought in her boss. I did not know him, and had only heard him described vaguely, but I knew immediately who the stranger was for whom Erica held the door open. The atmosphere changed at once. Some of the guests put their best foot forward, others retired into their shells. A cluster of people formed in my room, where the boss sat on the couch, the bolder ones around him, the shy ones in the background near the balcony doors and in the open doorway to the hall. I went quickly to make some fresh sandwiches and to turn the bowl upside down for the last of the punch. Back in my room, after serving the boss, I missed Erica. I found her in her room, where she was inexplicably busy tidying up. She emptied the ashtrays out the window onto the canal, shook up the pillows, and pulled chairs straight. She did not see me, and I withdrew silently. In my room the conversation was animated now and I looked for a place in the group. The boss was obviously enjoying the attention. He behaved like a father who "just came in to have a look at the young people." (The adolescents had been given the living room for a little party, while the parents arranged themselves as comfortably as possible upstairs in the bedroom, mother stretched out on the bed, with a cup of tea and a book on the night table, and father with his papers at the dressing table. After repeatedly exchanging glances of understanding at outbursts of gaiety downstairs, they decide that father should just go down, with an air of amiability and comradeship, to have a look.)

I must confess that the boss irritated me. He was *so* interested in what everybody had to say, and guided the conversation with *such* mannered tact and understanding, that I would have loved to put him in his place with a few well-chosen remarks. The discussion was about politics: the state and the individual versus the state and the masses—a subject that was discussed quite a lot in those days when all eyes were focused on Spain and Germany. I did not like the ideas of the boss. I waited for a defense of the individual, but nobody in the group seemed to feel the urge to protest. After half an hour I went to have another look for Erica.

Her door was ajar, the room was tidied up in Erica's manner, but Erica was not there. I glanced in the shower stall and the toilet, then in the kitchen, and even opened the kitchen door on the balcony. With a shock I realized she had gone out. I sat on her bed to wait for her. Maybe she had gone for some fresh air, or to get some cigarettes at an all-night bar.

Now and then I went back to my room, emptied ashtrays, casually piled together glasses and plates and carried them to the kitchen. Then I would return to Erica's room and lean out the window to look down the canal, hoping again and again that a late partygoer in the distance would turn out to be Erica. But she did not return, and when our gathering finally broke up, I closed the door to her room and said quietly that Erica had excused herself with a splitting headache, and had gone to bed. I let the people out, silently praying they would not meet Erica on the street. But she stayed away. I boiled some water, washed the dishes, tidied up, swept the room, and looked after the stoves. Toward morning, when I crept into bed exhausted, there was no trace of the party left; even the thick tobacco smoke had been driven outside, into the clear frosty night.

I lay shivering under my blankets. It was cold now in the apartment. Why had Erica left? Vague theories and possibilities crossed my mind. That pale face when she had shown in her boss came back to me continually, coupled with the memory of her excitement a few months ago on the way to Wies', when she had so unexpectedly dragged me across the street. Then my thoughts turned to Wies herself. Why had Erica not invited her? Was she perhaps spending the night with her? But why should she? I got out of bed and heated some milk. While I was slowly drinking this sedative, I heard Erica's key in the lock. Hastily I turned off the light. As I slid under the blankets for the second time, I heard her sneak upstairs.

Chapter Three

I DID not blame Erica for her strange behaviour, having promised myself I wouldn't. Anyway Ma arrived fairly early in the morning with wishes for the New Year, and talked incessantly. The General had had some friends in to celebrate, and Ma took a full hour to express her indignation at their attitude toward her: "They simply ignored me. I was just good enough to get the supper! Nothing but a maid!"

Immediately after she left Erica went to her room and did not appear again. In the afternoon I went out to visit friends and had dinner out. The New Year's Eve party was not mentioned again.

A few days afterwards, Erica presented me with a savings-bank book in her name. It was the inheritance, dwindled to five hundred guilders. I was to keep it for her.

"Why don't you keep the book yourself?" I asked, not much pleased with the job of treasurer she had thrown in my lap.

She ignored my question. "There'll be more money," she said casually. "I loaned some here and there."

Less than a week later she came to ask me for fifty guilders. "You mean you want the book back?" I asked, opening the desk drawer where I had put it. "Now listen, Erica, I really don't like this at all. It's ridiculous that I should keep your money for you. This way you have to ask me all the time. Keep the book yourself."

She refused stubbornly, and though she reddened, she did not explain. That same day I found the bank book back on my desk. We resumed the simple life we had led before

our windfall; the balance remained untouched. Suddenly
having to count in pennies again was a strange sensation.
Erica seemed to think it was rather amusing. She joked
about the seven lean years ahead of us. And really, in contrast to the sober existence our incomes allowed, the period
of abundance that lay behind us seemed longer than the few
weeks it had actually lasted.

As it was, we didn't have a lot, but we lived fairly well.
Erica seemed still to be paying off her debt to Ma. Her full
salary would have allowed her a more liberal way of life. As
before, she could deposit only a certain amount in the household fund, and since she never allowed me to put more than
she did into the bowl in the kitchen cupboard, I spent less of
my income than I might have. So I concluded that she had
not paid Ma back out of the inheritance. I did not understand
why; I suppose it was connected with the strange aspects of
the whole story. Erica's peculiar behaviour on the day she
got the money, and the fact that talkative Ma had never so
much as mentioned the gift on her later visit, indicated that
the legacy and the handing of it over to Erica were a kind of
epilogue to a family drama of which I then knew nothing.

We spent the winter months comfortably. Gradually I
started renewing old ties. I invited some friends to dinner
and went out a little more often. My efforts to take Erica into
our group succeeded only partially. She kept herself at a distance, and in the long run, as she began to evince criticism
and aversion, I did not take any further trouble. For equilib-
rium, I had even insisted on inviting Wies, but Erica did not
go further into the matter. Wies never came to see us and I
wondered whether Erica still saw her regularly.

Yet Erica and I spent a lot of time together; Erica
seemed to like it. Many evenings we sat reading in my room.
We also had fits of activity, when we would take up, say,

leathercraft, and be busy for weeks with awls and knives, and manufacture all kinds of useful and useless things. Or we would study graphology, or register for a course in fencing. These undertakings were spasmodic. Erica would get an idea, and after a short period of enthusiasm she would tire of it, and since I let myself be carried along by her in the first place, nay passion too cooled soon after she grew bored. Such quick enthusiasms were signs of Erica's restlessness, flights from a deeper-seated unrest, tasks she set herself in order not to get around to doing certain things she really wanted to do. I felt it even then, but only in a vague way which I could not express. A suspicion crossed my mind and would not let itself be formulated.

"What shall we do, Erica?" I would ask.

"What do you mean?" she said. "We don't have to do anything, do we? Why are you always bothering me about doing something?"

But at the same time she did not know what to do with herself. She would take down a book, leaf through it, take another one, offer to make tea, but not do it, eat an apple, lie down on the couch, write something that she would tear up in the kitchen, and finally, at her wits' end, after she had stood in front of the window for a half hour, would ask, "Shall we go to the movies?"

I did not understand why her work did not keep her busier. Journalism was, after all, an interesting profession, and I thought that reporters and feature writers also worked on assignments in the evening or gathered news. When I asked Erica about it, she was sarcastic. Oh yes, it was a romantic profession, but she hadn't got to the romance yet. In the foreign department a skill with scissors and paste was the highest virtue, and she was so good at it that they simply could not spare her.

"And your knowledge of languages," I said encourag-ingly. She shrugged her shoulders.

"What good does that do?" she said. "It's an ordinary office job, Bea. If I live long enough, I'll get around to art some day. That's what I really want—art and literature, but..." she finished with a discouraged gesture.

"I'm not a pusher," she added then. "Besides, I'm only twenty-one."

So she, too, was disappointed in her work, her profes-sion, and I was vexed at the shortsightedness of her employ-ers, who were surely underestimating her potentialities.

Yet that was not the cause of her restlessness, I knew. It lay deeper; it was connected with her true self, though she could certainly have found sublimation in her work for what troubled her emotionally.

Once, following a hunch, I asked her whether she was in love. She was positively shocked.

"Where did you get that idea? Me, in love?" The bitter lines at the sides of her mouth deepened. Then she seemed to have an inspiration: "Perhaps I *am* in love—God knows!"

I saw the idea amused her, and pursued it: "Your boss, perhaps?"

She laughed aloud. "Do you think I'm in love with *him*?"

I realized that question was childish and naive, and in spite of myself I started to laugh too. "I suppose you know best yourself," I said.

"Yes, one would indeed presume so!" Again she laughed uproariously, and I, tasting her sarcasm, retired again into my shell. "What did you think of him?" she asked in an effort to be serious and to force me once again into confi-dential confessions. Since the New Year's Eve party his name had not been mentioned, and the question was painful. She must have sensed my hesitation or read it in my face, for she cut off my reply with the statement that he was a very special person.

"That's quite possible," I said lamely.

"He is well informed," she went on almost apologetically. "I have lunch with him quite often." And as if that confession were the last straw, she grumbled that I asked the most insane questions, and left the room. So it was up to me to draw a conclusion, but I did not know which one. I did give some thought to it, recalling again Erica's schoolgirl behaviour during that evening walk in the autumn, but I didn't get much further than that. For some reason which I couldn't explain at all, I was unable to couple Erica and her chief in my mind, and since I never allowed myself—even in thought—to stick my nose into her personal affairs, I shook the whole matter off. The subject of men was not touched on again until a few weeks before Easter, when I met Bas. He was the manager of our branch in Rotterdam and at that time he used to come regularly to our office for conferences with my boss, who was under doctor's orders to live quietly and limit his activities to Amsterdam.

With Bas I had my first real affair. Before that there had been two others, and even though they don't really count, I still remember my surrender...and my misery after the breakup. They were short, violent relationships that had led to nothing but depression, followed by a temporary retreat to regain my self-esteem. Here in America I have had an adventure once in a while, but nothing has ever come of them. Men are like shadows in the background of my life. In the spotlight, where Erica played the leading role, there was no place for them.

When women of my age are asked, in confidential moments, why they never got married, they usually answer that they didn't feel like marriage, or that they never found

the right man. I give both these answers. Secretly I sometimes ask myself even now whether the combination of Bas
and me might not have contained all the elements for a
happy marriage. But those reflections serve no purpose.

I had known Bas already from his correspondence with
my boss as a level-headed and sympathetic man. Even a
business letter can give an impression of its writer. Along
with those qualities, which were attractive to me, I had con-
structed in my mind a physical image of him, which did
indeed fit in with reality. He was, it is true, a little shorter
than I had expected, but he did have that stoutness which
gives me confidence. He was prematurely gray, but his face
was still young, with the healthy colour of a man who has no
inner conflicts. I loved his broad well-formed hands, and
admired his sound teeth. Perhaps I singled out his physical
attractions in order to compare them with my own. I have
never been able to pride myself on my looks. Even then I
was what one would call colourless. I was always too thin
and too pale, my hair was straight and ash-blond, and I had
no interest or talent for choosing smart clothes. But I had
"good" hands, and as Erica said once, "magnificent teeth."

Bas reminded me of my father, and I felt so immediately
secure with him that when he took me to lunch I invited
him to come and visit me that same evening.

He stayed that night. I often still think with amazement
of the times when I have let myself be drawn so easily into
the extremest intimacies. I shared my bed with men who
were complete strangers to me. In the morning there would
be a stranger's face, and an embarrassment at the total rec-
ollection. Could it have been otherwise? And what did those
nights give me, really? But I suppose I was afraid that, once
a solid friendship had been established, I could not get
around to the physical relationship. Maybe I found it easier,

under the influence of drink and half-numbed with fatigue after an evening of groping and exploration, to let myself fall blindly. The pattern was always the same.

Yet it was only toward morning that I gave him—while listening sharply for sounds from behind the sliding doors—the satisfaction for which he had waited all night. My yielding was passive and more or less from a sense of obligation, but Bas was patient and he remained patient all through the nights he shared my bed.

As I think back to that episode, I realize clearly how vague feelings of guilt spoiled much of the happiness of that affair. My emotional ambiguity expressed itself in pointless apologies, concessions to both Bas and Erica, and a continuing sense of oppression. I have kept as my strongest memory what happened on Easter Sunday.

Bas had arrived on Good Friday evening. I had insisted on drawing Erica into our holiday plans. Even when Bas, on his arrival, surprised me with two theatre tickets which he had picked up on the way from the station, I asked, "What about Erica?" I ignored his expression of amazement, then his objections; he had to go and get a third ticket on Saturday morning whether he wanted to or not. Since I had insisted that we all sit together, he had to exchange the pair he had for three seats in a less desirable location.

Of course the situation bothered me. I was in a pretty difficult position, I told myself, for I was unable to see that my demands were unreasonable. Erica *belonged*; I was not going to leave her out during the holidays. It seemed unfair to me that Bas did not want to accept this even after my explanation. At the same time I was surprised at Erica's attitude. When I announced that the three of us were going to the theatre, she smiled and said, "All right," or "Nice,"—I have forgotten her exact words. I would have expected a protest, or at least some hesitation, at which I was ready to give her assurance that she "belonged." But here again she reacted differently, and nothing further was said about it.

Afterward, I tried to make it up to Bas; the strange sense of guilt pressed on me harder than ever that weekend. I went to extremes to please Bas. I remember that on Easter morning before he woke, I even gave my room a special clean-up, noiselessly, in stocking feet. I took him breakfast in bed, and forced him to stay there until I could put the festively arranged tray across his lap—although he would rather have got up to eat in the kitchen.

"You just stay in bed," I called at his protest, "it'll be ready in a minute!" Erica, in her pyjamas, was making the strong coffee without which she could never face the days and singing, "Mother I can't spare you..." It was one of those Dutch songs of which she knew all the words.

I had never been angry at her in all those months of living together; I had never found cause for impatience or objection. But now a furious rage rose in me. My heart pounded, my hands trembled, I didn't know what I was doing or what I had to do; I walked in confusion from the stove to the table.

"Erica!" I spat out, "Erica, stop it, Erica! Leave me alone!"

She sang on undisturbed: all the words, two verses. This is intolerable, I thought; I am getting out. We have to split up. This is no life for me. I can't bear her any longer!

What had happened, all of a sudden? Why did I feel a violent and overpowering aversion to Erica? I don't know whether I realized at that moment that the previous night was the cause of my guilt feeling and for my sudden fury. Probably the kaleidoscope of that day's events provided me with this insight later. I had not been able to give myself to Bas, not even after I had conquered my dislike. The embar-

rassment for Erica, who I knew was on the other side of the
doors, had been too strong, insurmountable. Bas's quiet
surprise, and his tactful questions later, had given me a
sleepless night—all the more unbearable because I was not
used to sharing my bed. Since I did not want to admit
insomnia to Bas, I forced myself to wait for the morning
motionless, simulating sleep. I wonder what went through
my head during those hours. Was I so naive that I thought
only of the next day and not of the basic conflict that lay
behind my inexplicable inhibition? I don't remember. But I
must have been surprised myself at my unreadiness, for I
had never suffered a similar incapacity with either of my
previous loves. Even though those two relationships had
ended only in heartache and disillusion, at least impotence
on my part was not to blame. It was rather the opposite; and
in each case it was I who suffered the cooling of the other's
passion. Long, painful weeks I spent asking myself why I
could not keep a man's interest.

Only when Erica had sung the last line of the street
song did she take notice of my anger. She put an affection-
ate hand on my neck and said soothingly, "Don't let it upset
you, my darling; I am a bitch!" There was sincere regret in
her voice, but I thought I also perceived a little triumph.
Just like a child, I thought; she has sung the song to the
end. Now I know better.

The whole morning she remained in the best of moods. In
the afternoon she went out. "I think I'll drop in on Wies," she
told me without her usual secrecy, "and have dinner at Ma's.
The General is out." She rolled her eyes upward to show how
she looked forward to that dinner. "See you at the theatre."

That afternoon I paid my debt to Bas (for that is how I
felt about it) and, ransomed for the moment, I enjoyed dinner with him at Dicker and Thys' and the theatre. Erica's

mood had changed; she was friendly but preoccupied. Afterward I went with Bas to the station. When I returned to the apartment Erica wasn't there, and I didn't hear her come home. Before I fell asleep, I wondered where she could be. I knew that she had spent the afternoon with Wies, and after that a few hours with her mother. I knew nothing about any other friends. What did she do when she stayed up until early morning? I reproached myself that Erica's first confidences about herself had made me want to know more. When she gives you a finger, you want the whole hand, I thought, dissatisfied with myself. I pressed my face into the pillow, and for a reason I did not know then, I cried.

The following evening Erica dawdled in the kitchen after the dishes were done. "When is Bas coming again?" she wanted to know.

"He's coming to the office on Thursday afternoon, but he has to go back the same night. Why?"

"No reason," she said, and then, jumping as it were from one ice-floe to another: "There is a new French film at the *Uitkijk*. How about it?"

"I'd like to, but..." I hesitated to tell her how tired I was. I had been longing for the end of the day; empty and listless somehow after the holidays, I looked forward to going to bed early.

"But what?" she asked, impatient. I foresaw difficulties, conflicts which I wanted to avoid at any price.

"Well, okay then. What time does it start?" I tried to make my voice sound cheerful.

"*Well, okay then!*" she mimicked. "When Bas is here you have enough energy for anything." So she had sensed my fatigue. But I realized too that she was trying to pick a fight at all cost. To gain time I closed the kitchen closet and wiped

the table top. Then I heard myself saying what I had
wanted to hold back.

"Listen, Erica, if Bas is beginning to make trouble
between us, we'd better break up."

"Who is making trouble?" Her childish reply annoyed
me. It was sickening that Erica should lower herself this
way; she wasn't like that.

"I'd as soon break off with Bas," I said before I fully
realized what the words meant.

Erica looked at me seriously. "Sorry, Bea," she said,
"Sorry. It's only..." she hesitated and then forcing herself,
she said, "It was so good just the two of us. But of course...
it's all nonsense. Don't think about it any more. I had a
lousy day yesterday. Ma...well, you know. And now, on top
of everything she has joined the National-Socialist Party—
passionately, of course." She laughed bitterly. "It's given me
a hangover. You go to bed, and I'll bring you a cup of tea in
a minute." Naturally this expression of outspoken warmth,
this backing down, this confession about Ma, had been too
much for her, and she pushed me roughly out of the
kitchen and into my room.

After that, the struggle went underground again. Erica
was superficially friendly when we were alone, and left
when Bas visited me. I had come to the conclusion that Bas
and I were not suited to each other; that he did not understand me properly; that he was really too old, too much of a
"business type" for me. Sexually, too, I disliked him. Even if
Erica stayed away on the nights when Bas came (and won-
dering where she was on those nights began to torture me
more and more) I could only participate in our love-life by
forcing myself. I had no need for it, I felt. In the end he
really could arouse me, but my passion did not come spon-
taneously. After all these years, I still have to laugh about it.

Bas, however, is so vague in my memory that I can no longer recollect him as a person, only as a shadow hovering over my life with Erica. Nevertheless, I am almost sure that I was fooling myself at the time; that under different circumstances our relationship might have been happy and harmonious, perhaps for life. I don't really blame Erica for it. Why should I?

The explosion came shortly before summer. We were making vacation plans; Erica was full of it. She had found an escape for her restlessness: we just had to go "somewhere." The remainder of her inheritance lay untouched at the bank, and the money I had saved for the sake of a fair division of our household budget, she said, must be spent on a trip abroad. Heaven knew whether this might not be our last chance, considering the international situation. It would have been all right with me, except that Bas had made some mention of a business trip he had to make to France, which he wanted to turn partly into a vacation trip with me. He was planning to buy a car anyway, and now he would postpone that until I could take my vacation and we would set out in the car together. In spite of the international situation—or perhaps because of it—everybody was talking about trips abroad. Half of the would-be travellers thought the risk too great; the other half boldly wanted to take the chance while there was still time. Should war break out, and it looked as though it might, then they would at least have seen something of France and Italy before those countries were destroyed by the madness. It was impossible to change the state of the world, said Bas: *après nous le deluge.*

I had not pursued the subject, but though I kept avoiding it, it preoccupied me. The idea appealed to me. In spite of the shortcomings of our relationship, I thought a motor

trip with Bas would be wonderful. Away from everything,
alone together, we would probably have a good time.
Basically, I thought, Bas is a fine man, he has an eye for
beauty, he enjoys it, he has taste and understanding...I had
a vision of the two of us in a little English car driving along
a country road in France—Bas would surely avoid the main
routes whenever possible—on one side hills of golden grain
and the other bordered by ancient farmhouses. I saw the
children playing in front of the doors, and the bench with
the mothers and grown-up daughters who sat with mend-
ing in their laps, watching us go by. We would pass a team of
oxen on their way to the stable, led by a half-grown boy who
drove the cruel flies from their flanks with a crueller stick.

We would lunch in a cool village bistro, the inevitable
bottle of *vin du pays* on the red-checked tablecloth; or in the
shade of a haystack, with the long crisp loaf of bread and the
cheese and the bottle of wine at our feet. These were characteristic dreams, inspired by stories of fortunate friends or
by travel posters. I had never been to France. The images
were always of rest and harmony, as was to be expected
when a happy couple wandered down Nature's paths! So
although I enjoyed my fantasies, I foresaw that Bas's idea—
yes, my vacation itself—would become the immediate cause
of a difficult situation: the choice between Bas and Erica.
Not that I saw it so concretely; oh no, there was nothing but
a thundercloud over a distant horizon, inferred rather than
actually seen. I avoided any discussion about the coming
vacation, with either Bas or Erica. When one of them
brought up the subject, I reacted with a vague "yes" or a
dreamy stare. When they tried to pin me down, I made up
reasons for my indecision. How could I make plans when
the office had not yet assigned vacations? Mine might just as
easily come in the autumn, or even in winter. What with my

boss's health...I made it sound as though I had nothing to say in the matter, as if others would decide and I could only wait for their decision. As a matter of fact I had first choice because I was private secretary to the director and because of my seniority with the company. Bas gave me some anxious moments by offering to go and have a word with my boss about it. I sidetracked him by pointing out that his intercession would betray the secret of our affair—something I wanted absolutely to avoid. I called it a breach of my privacy, and spoke so indignantly that he drew back with embarrassment and apologized for suggesting it.

Erica seemed to be determined to make me commit myself. As the summer approached she became more and more insistent. Soon not a day passed without her mentioning the vacation, making it sound increasingly more definite. Finally she made it seem as though we had decided to go together, and she would say something like, "Once we are in Belgium, we can easily get a lift to France," or "I can see us sitting on the Riviera!" Erica too had it in her head to go to France. During one of her monologues about "our" trip, I let myself be carried along so far that a remark about our limited finances slipped out: "How are you going to pay for all that? After all we only have five hundred guilders apiece, and besides, it would seem wiser to me if you didn't spend all your savings. I'd leave something in the bank, Erica."

She caught me right away. "So we are going?"

But I slipped off the hook. "I didn't say that. We're only talking about it, aren't we?" And then, helplessly, I pretended again that I had to wait for a decision at the office.

Erica ignored this. "All right, let's say that we count on four hundred guilders each. We'll hitchhike, of course; everybody does that now. It's ridiculous to pay so much for train fare. Besides, you see everything better from a car."

She was on dangerous ground here, considering Bas's plan to buy a car, and she immediately skipped to the point of destination, the Riviera. I did not feel at all like being at the mercy of miscellaneous car owners and drivers along the way, but I decided to save my protest for later. For later! Had I then decided to make the trip with Erica, and not with Bas? Whether I had or not, the real decision was made for me. Erica and Bas decided it—in my presence, but without me, since I was unable to control the situation. My self-possession left me; I let it happen that way. And even when they stood face to face and spat out the truth, I stayed in the background. I was so tired of the conflict—which I still refused to see in myself, and found only in them—that I let the storm pass over my head.

Chapter Four

As is usual when a bomb explodes, it took little to set it off. Again the holidays brought trouble; during Whitsuntide the pressure was unbearable. The extraordinary thing, looking back on it, is that I never went to Rotterdam. It would have been so simple if I had visited Bas in his home town, and spent Whitsunday and Monday with him. The idea occurred to me, but I didn't do it.

Bas lived in a furnished room, and I had told him firmly at the beginning of our affair that I did not like sneaking behind his landlady's back, or being confronted with her, even if as he said she permitted women visitors in the house. Bas had called me a little goose, but hadn't pressed the point. I didn't like the idea of a hotel any better. Heavens knows why, though at the same time I was considering living with him in French hotels I wouldn't have dreamed of spending the night with him in the same kind of lodging in Rotterdam. After all the travelling I've done in these years since being uprooted from Holland, I can't imagine such an objection. Maybe I was just provincial then, and stuffy. Though this may have been a factor, I rather believe the real reason was that I couldn't do without Erica, without the conflict, much as I suffered from it. It's strange what people do to themselves.

So during Whitsun, Bas was in Amsterdam. As a surprise he had a telephone put in my room the week before, so he could call me at night. Erica ignored the phone entirely, and I had not been really happy about it. Why now, at this point? I had thought; and it depressed me terribly

to realize that I considered our affair practically finished.
When Bas phoned me, as he did every night, I spoke with
difficulty, mumbling endearments to compensate for my
stilted conversation, which must have sounded like the dialogue in a cheap movie. "Are you tired?" he would ask. Once
he said my voice sounded as though I had a phobia about
telephones. "You've guessed it," was my hypocritical reply. I
knew Erica was sitting behind me, bent over a crossword
puzzle, but I sensed she was concentrating on the telephone
completely.

As Bas and I were having late Sunday breakfast, the
phone rang. It was Erica: "Are you doing anything special
tonight?"

"No...why? Not that I know of."

Her unexpected call, and her question, upset me so
much that I called aloud to Bas, "Are we doing anything
special tonight? It's Erica."

Through the open door I could just see him sitting at
the kitchen table; I saw him raise his eyebrows in surprise,
saw his hesitation, and how he stroked his forehead with a
tired gesture. He didn't answer, but I understood his gesture with a kind of shock, and mumbled some incoherent
words into the phone. Erica took them to mean that we had
no plans, and that her question had taken me unawares, but
that I was open to suggestion.

"I'm coming for a visit and I am bringing someone,"
she said, with that self-mockery in her voice I knew so well.

"Come ahead." By now I had recovered somewhat, and
I did not want her to think I was looking forward to her
visit; still I added that she was welcome. Back in the kitchen
I found Bas busy clearing the table. He had left my half-
finished cup of tea. I sat down to finish it, only because I
didn't know what to say. I didn't feel like any more tea.

"Strange, isn't it?" I forced myself to remark.

"I'm sick and tired of that girl!" It was the first time Bas had offered a straightforward opinion of Erica, and I was really grateful for it. His criticism relieved me. It broke the tension caused by his surface politeness and neutrality.

"She can't help it," I said to excuse Erica, "she doesn't know what to do with herself." Bas looked at me long and searchingly, without reproach, only with concern and sympathy for me.

"Do you, my little wife?" It was a name for the night, which in spite of everything I still treasured. The expression defined Bas's feeling for me in a way which evoked each time I heard it a doubt as to whether I didn't need and want the security it implied.

For a moment I was tempted to let myself go, to put my head down on the table for a good cry, and with that to surrender to Bas and so banish all conflict from my life. I didn't do it; I got up and took my cup to the sink. I let the moment pass. I had to go on alone, to the end of the long road.

That evening Erica turned up with her boss. As I saw him come up the stairs behind her, I was already conscious of Erica's almost childish effort to compete with me. I couldn't have imagined a worse combination than Bas and Erica's boss. I would never have brought those two together, but under the circumstances such consideration was not to be expected from Erica. John van der Lelie was very likely the only man in her circle available for the "competition." She led him in triumphantly. Now I feel a revulsion to all the petty thoughts, the miserable suspicions that went through my mind at that time. I couldn't help myself. At that period life was as lacking in design as a crazy quilt. It was a lesson for later; I have never again let things get so far out of hand.

Bas, good old Bas, even tried to help me that evening, though God knows he didn't have any reason to. I must have been a completely incompetent hostess, but already the next day I had forgotten what had been said, or how I had behaved, for in such a painful situation one acts as if in a dream—or rather in a fever. The senses are half-paralyzed, and one functions only externally while the emotions whirl madly inside. Sometimes I talked incessantly and without listening, rambling from one subject to another; at other times I sat silent while the conversation streamed over me. Bas was polite and acted as if he thought John van der Lelie held a lease on the wisdom of the ages. He did not contradict him, though I knew his interest was only pretended.

Erica behaved like an impresario, encouraging her chief and prompting him in his role of omniscient journalist. I had never seen her try so hard. At the same time she was obviously ill at ease, especially when Van der Lelie made it clear that he knew her inside out, that she was under his personal patronage, and that he considered it his chief mission to instruct her in life's mysteries. Over coffee and cake, I felt called upon to point out to Van der Lelie that Erica had quite a lot to offer, and that it seemed he was scandalously neglecting her possibilities. In reply, he put a fatherly hand on her knee and spoke of her youth and of the responsibilities of a journalist's life.

After Erica had seen him to the door, she came into my room and attacked me for "that stupid remark" about her work, and for my meddlesomeness. Bas took her by the shoulders and shook her gently, as one does with a child who misbehaves. But Erica tore herself free and asked him to spare her his fatherly intervention: "Bea and I can manage alone. She can take care of herself!"

She looked at me with a challenge, but I had turned

away and begun to undress for the night. Although we girls felt no embarrassment between ourselves, it was of course a different matter when Bas was there. Erica left the room. I had counted on that. So I did profit by Bas's presence in that way. Shortly afterward we heard her go downstairs and slam the front door with a resounding bang.

"I hope she catches up with Van der Lelie," said Bas dryly.

I had wanted to say that Erica was not going to him, but I let it go; I was too tired. Besides, how could I know where she did spend her nights from home?

Later, in bed, Bas took me in his arms as if nothing much had happened. I pretended sleep, and after a short time I heard his regular breathing. Once more I spent the hours awake. But this time I crept out of bed and waited in Erica's room for the daylight.

The following morning during our walk along the canal, Bas referred to the evening's conversation. It was then I understood he did realize the difficulties. He saw through the situation better than I—I can see that now. But because he was held back by an inborn reserve, by tact, and by the knowledge that I was groping in the dark, he did not try to help me further.

I would certainly suspect him of bias and prejudice, he said hesitantly, but he did want to offer me his opinion that Erica and I were not suited to each other, and that our living together would not make either of us happy. I couldn't think of any argument against that. He was right, but I could not possibly tell him that it had been different before he came into our life. "Our life," I thought, and when I realized I was thinking this way I had the irrevocable answer to my doubt. If I ever go back to Amsterdam, I will see landmarks of that Whit Monday walk. The path we chose along the ancient canals is imprinted on my retina as though the

visual impressions of that stroll were as important as the
confusion and pain I suffered.

When we were back at the apartment, I couldn't get the
front door open. My key did turn, but no matter how much
we fumbled and shook the door, it would not move. When I
rang, repeatedly, there was no response. I presumed Erica
was not at home, but I wanted to make quite sure. The
house remained dead-still. Since we were the only tenants
of the building, and the offices downstairs were closed for
the holiday, there was nothing to do but go and look for a
locksmith or a carpenter. With a great deal of persuasion we
succeeded in luring a plumber out of his house in a back
street. He managed to open the door, but in spite of the
generous reward Bas handed him, he refused to repair the
damage he had done in the process, or to reinstall the lock.
We climbed the stairs, and I asked Bas to go ahead in case of
prowlers. I was indeed a little worried, and I waited in the
upstairs hall. When Bas entered Erica's room I heard his
exclamation, "Well, goddammit!" and Erica's sleepy hello.

Without saying any more, Bas came out of her room
and walked past me into the kitchen. I found him at the sink
drinking a glass of water. He nodded his head toward Erica
and said between swallows, "Dead drunk."

Later he reproached Erica for having put the catch on
the door on purpose, and he ignored her apology that in
her intoxicated state she hadn't realized what she was
doing, and that she had not heard our ringing. The outburst, which started in the kitchen and reached its peak in
my room, degenerated into physical violence.

I had run into my room when Erica came to contradict
Bas's accusation that she was dead drunk. She sailed into
the hall, tousled and half-dazed. "Who is dead drunk, you
dirty liar?"

That's how the squabble started, and it ended with Bas's departure.

I sat on my couch in the corner, pressed back against the pillows, and I was not able even to look up from my clenched hands, let alone intervene when Erica in her rage went for Bas with a chair. The accusations, insults, and reproaches she flung at him he parried with sarcasm and insinuation. Yet I did not know exactly what he was saying to her; the words rebounded from my eardrums. Less than a month later the echo of his voice reverberated in my ears, and shortly thereafter I learned from Erica's own lips that his insinuations contained the truth.

I stayed neutral that day, and I lost Bas. I never saw him again. A few days later I heard at the office that he had offered his resignation. Only I knew the reason.

I felt relieved, and my hours of regret and self-reproach did not outweigh that relief. Besides, the plans for our vacation in France kept us busy. The preparations were drawn out endlessly. The anticipation was as highpitched as with a pair of teenagers undertaking a camping trip. Never had there been such solidarity between us. We had discussions that lasted hours. We fought good-naturedly over details. We studied catalogues and maps and enjoyed our fantasies like children. But when we left, late in July, fate was our companion. Erica could not be bound to a timetable. I know that with all our careful preparations we were going forward to the unknown. But I could not suspect that, for me, the anticipation was to be the high point. Even the passage of years has not erased the tortures of that vacation.

We had taken the train to Paris, but at Erica's insistence, to which I finally yielded, we were to hitchhike to Nice later. The days when we made our headquarters at the little hotel on the Left Bank passed all too quickly, although I was so exhausted by Erica's fast pace that I wasn't even looking forward to the Riviera. Erica rushed around like one possessed. She rested only when some café terrace pleased her, and even then she would turn her chair so that nothing could escape her. Often she would spring up to get a better view of something that drew her attention.

Although even now we had agreed to leave each other free, we were always together during the day. I soon noticed that Erica was much less a conventional tourist than I. Since I always need time to get used to new surroundings, I sought protection in the Baedeker. But here I raced around with her and felt, to tell the truth, secure in her company. She did not seem to object to my presence, though she did sometimes snap at me when I protested the never-slowing tempo, or begged for an hour of rest. We did see something of the museums, though Erica had little patience with a visit that lasted longer than an hour. She knew what paintings she wanted to see, and she knew where they were hanging; she would make straight for those pictures. There she would stand for a quarter of an hour, paying no attention to the other masterpieces around her. What she saw, she saw well, and that was enough for her.

When I protested her lack of a broader curiosity, she argued, "But I don't go to such places in Amsterdam either. That traipsing through museums is nothing but snobbery!" And with a wide gesture that took in the swarms of tourists around us, she added, "What do they know about art? They only go because it's the thing to do."

What interested her most was Paris itself, the Parisians, and especially life in Montmartre and Montparnasse. She seemed to have an unerring sense of direction, and we never lost time in finding our way. We roamed the streets for hours, and then by coincidence, it seemed, would arrive at the points of historic interest indicated in Baedeker. She would have nothing to do with men who tried to accost us. Whenever a man decided to take a chance on these two female tourists, he got a forceful rebuke. In spite of her limited French vocabulary—which incidentally was quite a bit more extensive than mine—Erica knew the *argot* of insult thoroughly. I suspected she got to know such expressions during her nocturnal wanderings.

Around midnight, as if by mutual agreement, we would say goodbye to each other and I would find my way back to the hotel, while Erica would go out "to paint the town" as she called it. How she could keep going with hardly any sleep was beyond me. Yet in the morning she was always up first, hammering on my door. I did not know when she came home—and even less where she spent the night hours. I presumed it was in the cafés of Montparnasse or Montmartre, but, as was my old habit, I did not permit myself to ask questions. She had set herself the goal of not wasting a minute, and after every adventure, or even during it, I felt her already longing for the next one. She wanted to see and experience everything, to taste every unknown drink, try every new dish, test every French custom, see the whole of Paris. She was feverishly busy, mentally as well as physically.

Later, much later, I understood that in those days she came to realize all she had missed in her own life: especially the abandoned enjoyment of the carefree person, without responsibilities, who doesn't have to account for herself to others. Though her circumstances had never allowed it, and her upbringing had barred such debonair behaviour, this kind of life was made for her. In those four days, for the first time, she threw the ballast overboard and blew the foghorn. She sailed through Paris on a pirate ship before the wind, the anchor cast away.

Our budget for Paris was gone after two days. When I saw our Riviera money dwindling too, I sent without telling Erica a telegram to Amsterdam for the remainder of my savings. She was totally blind to material limitations, and I did not want to break the spell.

Chapter Five

LITTLE wonder that I no longer have a clear memory of our adventures in Paris. There was too much pressure, too much of everything. I just kept trotting along. Of course I do remember the afternoon we met Judy. It was in a restaurant. We hadn't had a chance for breakfast, and when we finally settled down in a little bistro it was almost three o'clock. I was sick with hunger, but I hadn't been able to put the brakes on Erica long enough to end the gnawing in my stomach.

The restaurant was empty except for the young woman who sat at a corner table opposite ours and two provincial couples at the next table, who were obviously taking the trip for which they had saved a decade. I saw that the girl, an American, had started a conversation with the others. She was especially charming to the men and I noticed with amusement that for them the green light of "Paris adventure" was beginning to flicker alluringly. Their eager response was immediately smothered by their plump, firm wives who from experience recognized the ominous signs: twinkling eyes, reddening necks and agitated breathing. The women froze visibly and soon insisted on leaving with their husbands in tow.

It was evident that the young woman was American from her clothes and the way she wore her hair and make-up. She had style, as Erica remarked emphatically, and certainly "knew her way around." The difference between her striking costume and the simple coats of the other women was painful, and I knew that Erica and I too looked like provincials beside her. On closer examination, one discovers that this kind of bohemian young American woman isn't really well-groomed. But her casual chic is meant to capture attention. Erica found it attractive and interesting.

When the two couples left, the American stared at us for a moment and then came straight to us. "Do you mind if I sit down?" she asked without a trace of timidity. "I feel lonesome."

Erica blushed, but immediately pulled out a chair for her. In ten minutes, she had given us a rough sketch of her situation. She was alone in Paris; she was divorcing her husband who, notwithstanding, was giving her this trip to Europe through a travel bureau whose legal affairs he handled. In spite of the man's generosity, she didn't have a good word to say for him.

I was astounded at such frankness and took an immediate dislike to her, but Erica seemed to be fascinated. And thus it happened that that afternoon Judy became the third party. Or rather, I must confess that soon a change took place and I found myself the third party. Often it was on the tip of my tongue to take leave of them, but I stayed and said nothing. Within an hour Erica and Judy were already walking hand in hand, or with their arms around each other's shoulders. I couldn't believe what I saw, but I plodded along resignedly.

Their friendship was short but violent. The breakup came before dinner-time with such a vulgar quarrel that even the preoccupied Parisian passers-by gave their attention to it. After a "Drop dead!" from Judy and an equally explicit curse from Erica, our ways parted. It had all started at the handbag counter of Le Printemps, where Judy had wanted to buy a gift for Erica. I didn't know the details, since, as soon as the offer was made, I had gone discreetly to the other end of the counter, ostensibly to look at silk scarves.

Back in the street, Erica fell into a brisk pace. She was visibly upset, and smoked one cigarette after the other as we went on in silence.

"Must have been a lot of fun for you!" she said suddenly.

"Not exactly. What was the matter?"

"You wouldn't understand."

All through the afternoon I had felt like a whipped dog, and that remark climaxed it. At the other side of the square we were crossing, I saw an entrance to the Metro. Without a word I made for it, and took a train to the hotel. I had still heard Erica calling my name, but I ignored it. During the ride I sank into a depression that blinded me to any silver lining. Perhaps I saw salvation in action, for when I got to my room I started packing in a furious haste. I imagined then that I was possessed by the need to flee from Erica—to be gone before she could reach the hotel. Later it was clear to me what I really desired: Erica's worry about me, her anxiety, and her repentance when she found me gone.

The phrase "loss of self-respect" drummed in my mind and left no room for constructive thought. In no time I had dragged my luggage down the stairs. I could not wait for the elevator; in that barred cage that still jolted and jerked its way up the shaft, I would be doomed to inaction. I had to keep moving to save myself from choking despair.

I paid my own bill, and only shook my head when Madame handed me the bill for Erica's room. Though I took care of finances and knew that Erica had hardly any money with her, I did not pay it. At the door I called back, "*Mon amie reviendra pour ses bagages et l'addition!*" It was the only time I ever reacted to Erica's behaviour with instinctive revenge. I still admire it.

Only when I stood at the curb opposite the hotel, waiting for a taxi, did I come to my senses enough to wonder where I would go. I lacked the courage to travel alone. Back to Holland, I decided.

At that moment I saw Erica hurrying toward the hotel. I made myself as small as possible behind a tree, but she was so intent on her purpose that she didn't look up or back. I stayed where I was. Several empty taxis passed, but I didn't call one of them. Probably I stood there for only a short time, but those minutes were an eternity in which I realized that there was not much left of the willpower I had been so proud of. In bitter self-contempt I drew up the balance sheet. The image of Bas and Erica facing each other in my room on that Whit Monday came to me with the words Bas spoke, the truth of which I now guessed: "Watch yourself, your affection for Bea is based on unhealthy emotions. You are a dangerous girl."

When Erica came out of the hotel and searched along the street, I fled from those words, back to Erica. She took my luggage and nudged me gently with her shoulder in the direction of a small bistro on the corner. Then I cried, with tight painful sobs.

Dramas like this, which now seem so childish and ridiculous, occurred several other times during the trip. It seemed that Judy was pursuing us; in my more lucid and reasoning moments, I knew it was true. Sometimes, when I chose to let self-deception carry me away, I could argue that our itinerary simply ran parallel to hers—since after all we were following the usual route to the South. For I told myself then that Erica, in spite of herself and only through the fault of others, put me in painful and humiliating situations. On that illusion my strength was based. I am grateful for it, because only on that basis could I later establish my self-respect and my resignation. Now, after all these years, it is no longer important.

Erica's actions have long since taken on a different meaning for me.

Erica recognized Judy in the Cathedral of Chartres. Judy was wandering about bored, disguised behind odd-shaped red-framed sunglasses which made her look like a harlequin. In retrospect, it is worth a smile that I then saw a symbolic meaning in the depiction of the Christ, carved from wood centuries ago by magical hands, which drew my attention that morning even more than the famous windows. I felt like the martyr, while Erica and Judy sat on a church bench making up their quarrel of yesterday. And I was so inspired by the wooden images that I turned the other cheek, and we continued our trip in Judy's little Renault. At Tours again, our ways parted in a second quarrel. This time I was the cause, and though I am sure Erica would rather have taken Judy's side, she stuck by me. What is more, she attacked Judy with a vehemence that overwhelmed me. Within a very few weeks I had now experienced three of these outbursts, and each time I had been amazed at the violence of her eruptions. Erica's face was a mask of hate; behind her words it seemed there was a steam boiler on the point of exploding. I felt that she gave expression to much more than she could feel at the moment, more than the incident justified.

During the quarrels with Judy I had to suppress not only my amazement, but also a sense of hilarity. It was really ridiculous, the emotion they displayed. Only later I learned that women in Erica's situation always swing to extremes, in love as well as in animosity. In their relationship, they were like little girls who at one moment hit and scratch, and at the next are closely entwined, confiding deep secrets and swearing eternal friendship. But then I still had to get used to it. In Tours, I had tipped the scales by refusing to have lunch in

the most expensive restaurant and by rejecting Judy's offer
to treat us. Our budget was calculated to allow for bread,
cheese, and wine along the road, or if necessary, in a village
inn, and only I knew where the money for those simple
meals was coming from. Even though I would not bare the
secret of our strengthened capital, I didn't want to spend my
own money in needless dissipation to keep up with Judy.
And I refused to take advantage of Judy's financial position.

As we continued our trip alone in the car of an English
couple, Erica did call me a wet blanket and a bluestocking,
but I suppose it was meant as a joke. We had a wonderful
trip. The couple, though of course full of English reserve,
turned out to be friendly and thoughtful. They took us as
far as Nice. We had to be at their hotel at a certain hour in
the morning for the departure, but during the three days of
the ride they left us completely free. They just provided us
with the seats in their car, without obligation. We really had
luck, and those three days were ideal.

In Nice, things went wrong again. Erica developed a
passion for roulette—a passion I did not share, but in fact
feared. Still I went with her and occupied myself by watching and philosophizing. Judy turned up in the gaming
room, and after she and Erica had fallen into each other's
arms they appeared again inseparable. I must admit that
her Renault was a great advantage. We saw the entire coast,
up to the Italian border, and by isolating myself, I kept out
of trouble. I was the neutral spectator, a role into which I
forced myself, and which I maintained with constant self-
discipline in spite of some miserable moments. Only that
way was the expedition possible and my position irre-
proachable. To all appearances I was entirely free of Erica,
and I don't believe she noticed anything of my inner struggle. Now and then she threw me a crust of friendship, which

I accepted tacitly. She made these brief overtures doubtless because at those moments she needed a witness who could confirm the reality of her wonderful experiences. After a day or two of practice I was able to isolate myself when we arrived at a certain town or landmark. We would agree on an hour for departure and I would go on my own reconnaissance trip. Erica and Judy, of course, could seldom be bothered keeping track of the time, and usually I spent hours waiting. But that way at least I saw what interested or attracted me without the torment of their company.

The evenings were a special problem because the two of them could not be kept out of the gambling rooms. Sometimes we had to drive for miles to the nearest Casino; Erica and Judy went inside while I wandered around outside. Later I could tell from their conversation whether they had won or lost. It was in this way, too, that I learned Judy was providing Erica with gambling money.

The night hours alone in my hotel room, cool and fragrant as they were, always lasted too long for me. I couldn't sleep; even the sedative I got from a druggist in Nice, after a stammering explanation, did not help.

Since we had only sixteen days vacation and Erica still wanted to see "everything," there was nothing but endless driving, driving. When I think now of the Côte d'Azur, I still get an impression of the gray Renault racing ceaselessly along the boulevards with Judy at the wheel, Erica beside her, I in the back. The "rest cure" that had appealed to me so much in Paris was in reality—and is in my memory—nothing but a merry-go-round. I am sure that I must have lain for hours on the beach, but I can't picture it any more. Sometimes I saw Erica and Judy there. They lay baking in the sun, their arms around each other; or they threw a beach ball back and forth, shouting, happy as schoolgirls.

Their bodies in the brief French bathing suits were browned and glistening with oil. When they saw me, they threw me a casual "Hello," but most of the time I managed to pass them unseen. After they once ignored me on a café terrace, I began to avoid the sophisticated boulevards. Blinded by the glaring sun, and being suddenly in the shadow of the marquee, I had not recognized them at first. I was standing opposite a large circle of what I judged to be American and French women, who sat drinking Pernod with studied boredom. There was a husky middle-aged virago, dressed in a seaman's sweater, and six young girls, dressed and coiffed with the masculine touches meant to isolate them from ordinary women. Looking around the circle, I discovered Erica and Judy among them. I saw the quick warning glance they exchanged, and then the vague smile from Erica that took the place of a greeting. I turned in my tracks and left hurriedly, and the humiliation of that retreat stayed with me for a long time.

After this, the boulevards were for me only a way of getting to the beach; for the rest I limited myself to seeing the villages and watering-places themselves. But the long walks in Antibes, in Cagnes, in St. Paul, in Villefranche, and all the other places—I see them now as a movie spectator would, a spectator who looks at a documentary film with little attention to the actor who has to climb the cathedral steps or pose at the town-hall gate to animate the picture...still less to what that actor thinks or feels in spite of his cheerful expression and his quick step.

When the day of departure came, Erica told me bluntly that she was staying a little longer. Judy was present, and since she stared a challenge at me, I did not react.

"Call the paper and tell them I'm deathly ill," said Erica, "Tell them anything, I don't care what!"

It was true that she didn't care, and the decision not to return on time didn't bother her in the least. Though she had known all along when her vacation must end, and had filled her days to the bursting point, she simply could not stop. As a concession to me, she persuaded Judy to take me to the station in Nice. So she did feel somewhat guilty toward me, but I was too miserable to think about that. After an indifferent goodbye in front of the station, they drove away and I followed the porter inside.

Chapter Six

ERICA stayed away until the end of August. She later confessed to me that it was only Judy's hurried departure for America because of the impending war that had forced her to return to Amsterdam. In the meantime I had heard nothing from her. Three times a day, I looked in vain in the mail box for a letter, or even a postcard. I strained my ears to hear the first delivery in the morning. Sometimes, when my restlessness was too strong, I went home during lunch hour for the midday mail; and in the evening I sat up listening for the postman. As the international crisis worsened, and the fear of a German invasion grew, my worry about Erica increased too. What the crisis actually did was to furnish an excuse for my concern, and to give me a pretext for talking to friends and colleagues at the office about Erica's staying away. But in reality, the world around me could have exploded without worrying me more than the conflict between Erica and me. I was completely absorbed by personal difficulties. After all, it is like that: war often offers an escape or an alibi for the human being at the end of his rope, who can see no help in the future and secretly hopes for an external catastrophe to put an end to the unbearable situation.

During the preceding year, the world had drifted irrevocably to the edge of the precipice, but the shocking events in Spain, Austria, Munich, and Asia had hardly touched me. I had moved like a riding horse in training; blinkers prevented me from seeing anything but Erica, who was trotting in front of me, whom I could not, and was not allowed, to overtake. Now I found an outlet for my tormenting thoughts, through telling everybody how I worried about Erica's staying away, and linking it to the international crisis. I even went so far in my self-deception as to telephone the paper. Van der Lelie advised me to get the help of the consul in Nice. He offered to send the telegram himself; perhaps he knew whether Erica had been admitted to a hospital. "I had been intending to phone you myself," he said importantly. "I'm very worried too." So he had swallowed the story that Erica was ill! On August 29, when the general mobilization was announced, I was near a nervous breakdown. But the next afternoon at one o'clock, Erica was standing before me. She had come by plane, and with an excited report about her first flight, she took the emotion out of our reunion. A little later she ran down the stairs on her way to the office. Suddenly she was in a hurry to be on time. And a few moments later, as I was walking along the canal to the streetcar, I saw her dashing around the corner on her bicycle as though she had never been away.

That night, as formerly, I cooked the meal, and as she sat down at the table she said, "I behaved like a beast, Bea, but I couldn't help it. It was *too* lovely! You'd better forget the whole thing, if you can. And if you can't, you'd better tell me now. Don't keep looking at me with those calf-eyes!"

With that, the matter was settled for her. I choked down my food as well as I could and, with the excuse that I had a date, I left the house immediately after doing the dishes. I roamed the ancient part of the city until midnight and when I came home I felt I had conquered my emotional strife. Now I can confess that I was so happy about Erica's return, the struggle was the purest make-believe. It was no more than a comedy I performed for myself and to myself, to put a proper end to the drama.

Our life resumed its normal course. A few times a week a thick envelope arrived from America, and Erica spent much time in correspondence. That fall she was apparently able to live a full life. Perhaps she was still existing on the satisfaction of the summer; perhaps the excitement and anxiety of the tense political situation diverted her. Of course her work at the paper had become more important. So much was happening, within and beyond the borders, that Van der Lelie couldn't help but exploit Erica's talents. She often worked overtime; in October she was put on the roster for the night shift. She always brought home exciting stories, and for the first time since I had known her she had an outspoken opinion about fascism and the Nazis.

As was to be expected, she swung to the far extreme, and often the apartment reverberated with the violence of her speeches. Her hatred for the Germans was boundless, and Ma, as the handiest exponent of the opposite view, received the brunt of it: "Now listen to this, Bea...that stupid woman...it's fantastic...she says the salvation of Europe is in Hitler's hands—and you should hear her go on about the Jews! Because Pa is one, I suppose. Didn't I ever tell you that? Oh yes, I'm half...But anyway, maybe it isn't even that, although she'd gladly see him drop dead. She's stupid, Bea, and disappointed...well, you know the sort to run with that gang. And that's my mother!" Then in conclusion: "She can't come here any more, don't forget!"

I hadn't seen Ma in months anyway, and it didn't look as though her political activities would leave her much time to visit her daughter. It did not occur to Erica that, should she make such a visit, I couldn't keep her out. And the curious thing was that apparently she herself did visit her mother. Probably she could not resist the temptation to tell Ma the blunt truth, to air her long-suppressed contempt under the

guise of political differences. The humorous anecdotes had
stopped for good. Now Erica would sometimes let slip incidents about the past which were not open to any cheerful
interpretation. How much scorn, hate, and bottled-up
aggression had been hidden in her previous mockery and
jokes, I learned from Erica's reaction to Ma as a National
Socialist. Those stormy visits to her mother seemed to give
Erica satisfaction.

In November she joined a society whose members travelled to the border to meet Jewish refugee children from
Germany. She also attended political meetings, including
those of the Dutch Nazis, where she participated in the
heckling to such an extent that, as she told me with childish
pride, she was occasionally thrown out.

"I hope Ma saw that!" she would say.

"Was she there?" I asked.

"I suppose so. That woman has gone completely crazy."

"What does the General say about it?"

"What a question! He's the same way, of course. You
know him."

Thus Erica divided mankind into the good and the
National Socialists, and she could place everybody. "That's a
potential one," she would declare about someone. "Either
he's already wrong, or he's going to be." Many an innocent
citizen was brought under suspicion, but in some cases she
hit the nail on the head.

I felt a violent aversion to all the excitement and kept
aloof. Yet sometimes I did let myself be persuaded to do
some administrative work that Erica undertook but never
finished, or to read the books and pamphlets she brought
home. I have never taken to political agitation. Even then I
had little faith in humanity, and now that I am in my forties
I know for sure that men who stand on soapboxes have

more hate than goodwill within them. And, as was the case with Erica at the time, they are often eager to populate the lonely steppes with their enemies and their comrades.

Whenever I expressed myself in this way, I had to pay the price. Once Erica flung in my face that I always thought the worst of people, that I had no love. They were merciless words, and they kept me worried for days. I had to admit that I was changed, embittered; secretly I blamed Erica for it.

But it was not long before Erica's political ambitions came to an end. Her love for her fellow men was not equal to Van der Lelie's intrigues, and she threw down her weapons as readily as she had taken them up. Suddenly she was at home again, and she no longer said a word about the dangers of Nazism. Only after about a week did she give me an explanation, bit by bit.

It did not surprise me that Van der Lelie had turned out to be a Nazi; I thought the black shirt suited him admirably. In the city there were already rumours about the sympathies of the newspaper's management. Van der Lelie was risking nothing when he gave her the choice between her political activity and her job. At that point I took the offensive, and expressed surprise that she had given in so easily. At first she put forth all kinds of excuses. Van der Lelie had threatened to make it impossible for her to get work elsewhere. He would not give her references, or he would give her bad references, or he would warn others against her. If she got a job with another paper she would have to start from the beginning again, and she would not earn enough. There were no other journalistic jobs open to women; in politics they could manage without her. And finally, "What does it matter anyway?"

Of course I could not accept these pretexts, but I let it go at that. Erica looked so miserable and was so depressed that I left her in peace. She spent a Sunday in bed, a flight from reality she had not taken for a long time. This state of mind, so inexplicable in her, kept me awake at night; I could not make head or tail of it. Was she, after all, still in love with Van der Lelie, and had she capitulated so as not to lose his interest? Or had the disillusion been too much for her when the man developed into a National Socialist? Then what a child she must still be!

In those days Wies telephoned repeatedly. She had never called before, so far as I knew. She wanted to know where Erica was, and when she would be home and whether I had seen her by any chance. I answered as well as I could, and gave Erica her messages; she showed little interest in them. Once, when a call came while she was at home, she signalled frantically that she wasn't there. At the first phone call I had thought: so she does still see Wies. From the next few calls I concluded that she must have turned to Wies for aid and comfort in this crisis. But when Erica showed she wanted to avoid Wies, I did not understand anything any more. How naive I was! But how could I have suspected then that Van der Lelie had taken advantage of what he thought he knew about the relationship between Wies and Erica? Blackmail was then still beyond my horizon. It was a concept, a word I had come across, but one that had no place in my vocabulary. From my position I could not see that Erica, so many years younger than I, so childlike with her whims and her immature remarks, Erica with her shiny boy's haircut and her sloppy boy's shirts and her sock-clad legs, had exposed herself to a man with a knife up his sleeve.

After a week or two, Erica instructed me to tell Wies that she was busy, but would write to her. When I did this, there was a short silence and then a sneering laugh at the other end of the line. That was the end. I heard Wies' name mentioned once more, months later, when Erica no longer had any secrets from me.

"Take that case with Wies," Erica said, "it was fairly innocent, sexually speaking, though we often slept together in the same bed. At that time I wasn't doing that sort of thing yet. But Van der Lelie scared me to death. I didn't dare meet Wies again. He had seen through me before I had even seen through myself. When he accused me, it was a kind of revelation. Jesus, I'll never forget those weeks!"

And what about Judy?" I had asked.

"I was naive, Bea. For Judy those things were done for a thrill. She could take them or leave them. She made it an adventure for me. You can't understand that, Bea."

Erica would never forget those weeks, and neither would I. She looked as if she were ill—yellow-pale, with dark rings under her eyes. The lines under her eyes really set themselves during that time, and afterward her skin showed fine wrinkles. She ate hardly anything, and as far as I knew she didn't sleep at all.

Whenever my worry woke me, I saw the light through the sliding doors. I could not help her. Our conversation was limited to my encouraging her to eat and to the weather, to which she replied respectively with a growl and a word or two. Gradually her restlessness gave way to depression. Now Erica did not look for diversion. She did her work at the paper, and in her free hours she hung around the flat. The letters from America stopped coming, and Erica, at least at home, didn't touch the pen. She lay on her bed, she looked out of her window for hours, she seemed afraid to leave the house.

Though I too felt depressed, now and then I spent evenings away from home. The atmosphere was unbearable; sometimes I couldn't stand it any longer. But when I went out, I felt uneasy and longed for the apartment. At last, of course, Erica cheered up. Her desire for variety and relaxation was reawakened and once again she looked for a change.

Chapter Seven

Not long afterward, on a Sunday in October, I thought how she was like a bird that cannot decide where to alight—under the roof of a house, where there are human faces behind the windows, and a voice, a laugh, an unfamiliar sound warns of caution; or in this tree or that; perhaps in the eaves of the shed; or rather yet, safely in the wood. A flying to and fro, a frightened skittering, a restless fluttering, then floating gracefully away again, turning about to start the deliberation over again.

We had gone out into the dunes. It was already cold, and I had found a cove sheltered by a fisherman's dwelling, while Erica stood on the beach looking out across the sea. A late blackbird, lost here on the shore, held my attention for a while, and it was this bird that suggested the comparison.

"You know," Erica said when she came back, "we really don't live right. We should rent a little house on the ocean, give up the apartment, and commute to work."

"Yes," I said, "a good idea." I could say it easily, for in a short while she would certainly have forgotten the idea. I didn't have to go into it any further. Wasn't it always like that: suggestions that were never acted on? Plans, restlessness, a waiting for...yes, for what?

But this time I had miscalculated. I had not even paid any attention to Erica's attitude in the week following that Sunday. I had of course noticed her somewhat more cheerful mood; I had only considered myself lucky to have an atmosphere of peace and harmony in the house for a few days at least, and to know that she was happy. On Saturday she announced that she was going out on Sunday, the whole day, and that I was not to count on her. As usual I didn't ask any questions, and when I woke at ten on Sunday she had disappeared.

I spent the morning alone, treated myself to breakfast in bed, wrote some letters, read, and enjoyed the quiet. But in the afternoon, in the Rijksmuseum, among the couples and the families shuffling past the paintings and the suits of armour, a singularly lonely feeling came over me. I thought of Erica. I missed her, but I brusquely pushed back that sentiment. I had forced myself to come to the museum; after all, one has to *do* something. One shouldn't spend the whole day at home. There under the high-arched ceilings, among people enjoying the company of family or friends—I then considered that ideal!—I asked myself why I hadn't stayed home in the room that was familiar to me, and wrapped myself in its security. Why should I force myself? Was the compulsion to activity beginning to torment me, too? Or was I afraid of what Erica might say finding I had sat at home all day Sunday; afraid of her disapproval and a certain contempt which at the time I thought I could always notice?

The choking sense of loneliness that took me by the throat then was stronger even than during my solitary walks through the French coastal villages. While I looked at the Rembrandts and Vermeers, trying to seem interested, the canvasses might as well have been blank. I was strongly conscious of the people around me. I envied and feared them because they intensified my overwrought state of mind. I was indeed a pitiful figure, and I had probably already begun to match the picture Erica would draw for me hours later.

About seven, just as I was feeding myself some warmed-over food from a pan at the kitchen table, Erica came stomping up the stairs. So she is still cheerful, I thought at once, and probably full of gay stories.

"Done! Settled!" she said as she dropped into a kitchen chair.

"Have you eaten?" I asked, one hand reaching for the bread box.

"Much too excited. I'll eat later. Let it go. We have an apartment at the sea. In Egmond! Terrific luck!"

"A what? Where?" I was so completely overwhelmed that my hand continued mechanically to take the loaf of bread from the box, then started to search for a knife in the drawer.

"We are going to live at Egmond on the Sea," she said. "Give me some money right away. I have to send a deposit first thing tomorrow. I've already got the key. Very nice people; they trusted me just like that." From her jacket pocket she drew a brand-new key, and held it shining before me. "They are still building, almost finished. We can move in next month."

This, then, was a completely rash action following the period of depression. An act of despair, I said to myself, a wild leap after the period of inertia that she could bear no longer.

Stunned, I sank onto the other kitchen chair. "My God, Erica...how can you?" But I went no further. She seemed so happy. The bird had finally decided on a resting place. I could not discourage her, not now. Perhaps some cautious questions in a few hours to recall her to reality later in the evening. Egmond on the Sea, I thought frantically...it was no suburb, not in commuting distance...how far was the train ride from Amsterdam? Was there a connection, maybe a bus...? The lease here—how could we get rid of this apartment?

"Something wrong again?" she began. "Do you always
have to be a killjoy? Miss Milquetoast again! You have no
courage, not a grain of it. This isn't life!" A gesture of her
arm took in the little kitchen, the bread knife I still held in
my hand. "Life is too short. You must take advantage of it."
That theme seemed to please her, and she pursued it, working herself up. "We sit here like two parakeets on a perch.
Every day is the same. We're not so young any more; how
many years have we wasted already? Especially you; after all
you're older than I am. What do you get out of it? Office.
And there you sit with your bread knife in your little kitchen
with the red-checked ruffles at the window and the red-
checked sailcloth on the table. Lovely, that fresh red! So
very nice! And Wednesday night you're invited to Dottie
and Max's, with their whining brats. They'll serve you pan-
cakes for dessert—to top a charming evening. Saturday
nights we go to the movies and Sundays we go for a walk.
Look at you in your Sunday outfit like new, with that daring
scarf. Life can be beautiful, full of excitement and cups of
tea. You're stifling me. Before I know it I'll be just like you.
I won't even notice it myself. Two old maids in a cosy
upstairs apartment." She cursed suddenly and struck her
fist on the table. "I have to get out. Maybe I should get away
from you. This is not for me." Then, remembering the new
venture: "We're going to Egmond. I'll give it a chance. At
least it's something."

The edge of the bread knife cut painfully into my forefinger; I had let my hand slide down the blade during her
tirade. I licked off a drop of blood, sucked at the finger.
What now...what could I say? "Now, Erica..." I began soothingly. But she took the knife from my hand and started to
make her supper with impatient gestures. Two chunks of
bread, a lump of cheese, a glass of beer.

"Why don't you let me...?" I arose from my chair. At that
she threw down everything, looked at me with hate in her
eyes, and stalked out of the kitchen. I sat still for a while,
with the slamming of the door and the beat of my heart
sounding in my ears.

Later as I paced nervously in my room, I heard her
busy again in the kitchen. So she was hungry—and I had to
leave her alone. The dainty sandwiches with the cold steak
I had saved from the evening before, the pickles and sliced
tomato, everything tastefully arranged on a cheerful
plate—and, as a surprise, the pastries I had bought on my
way home from the museum...that's the way I had wanted
to do it. But I shouldn't. I must not spoil her like that, and
force my care on her. No wonder she was angry. I ought to
leave her free in that respect too.

Then again I saw myself in the museum, and the echo
of the pain I felt there wove sickly through my stomach.
Involuntarily my fingers went to my new scarf. Then tight
stifled sobs gave me some relief. Erica had struck hard at
me. A silk scarf from Liberty's, really much too expensive,
that I had thought would brighten last winter's dark blue
dress. How clearly I saw myself wandering at the museum!
"One must *do* something, after all." But I had only exposed
myself to needless torment, to loneliness, to the wretched
reaction of the overwrought. How had I changed so? What
had happened to me? I did not understand it then.

So we moved to Egmond on the Sea. I have forgotten
the details of what happened in the three weeks that passed
before we drove to our new home in a truck. But I can still
see myself sitting there on top of the load, on a folded
horse-blanket, our possessions around me, a stale-smelling
tarpaulin around my head and shoulders to protect me
from the drizzle...again helplessly delivered into a leaden

depression that seemed to descend on the clattering truck along with the rain. Erica sat in front between the movers, with a girl named Dolly on her lap—a girl I had never met before, never even heard about. They seemed to be enjoying themselves. Now and then their laughter blew toward me. I felt like a piece of furniture, dragged along in Erica's flight from herself.

Tired as I was with the tension and the silent animosity that prevailed before I had finally given in, exhausted with the business about the Amsterdam apartment and the packing, the complications of country living seemed to me insurmountable. Halfway through the trip, Erica stopped the truck and came up with an offer to change seats. I refused; I was all right where I was and enjoyed the unlimited view: "Just like a movie, Erica, everything rolls past. Very nice!" No, I wasn't going to break up this "adventure." Such a comedy I played so well by then that Erica, completely convinced and happy at my reaction, climbed in front again.

I really should enjoy it, I told myself. The landscape, low and dyked in, so typically Dutch, now in a broad panorama unbroken by train or car windows was indeed impressive, and rather more beautiful in the gray weather. My effort to concentrate on all this failed completely. The unexpected presence of this Dolly had unnerved and irritated me so much that my last ounce of courage went down the drain. Why had Erica asked her along? She was certainly not the type one might ask to help with moving, or who, conscious of her own efficiency, offers such services. Yet she had appeared promptly at seven that morning. She had not lifted a finger, but brought me to despair with her quasi-worldly remarks and her anecdotes about people I did not know. And after we arrived in Egmond she made

herself comfortable in an easy chair. I had to go out for coffee; she did not contribute even that small service. As I hurried through the rain looking for a café, I wondered
whether I should expect another "Judy affair" with Dolly. At
that moment I saw the future through pitch-black glasses,
so I was quite prepared to find Dolly a permanent guest, or
to sit alone myself in Egmond while Erica enjoyed herself
with Dolly in Amsterdam. What did she see in her? In my
low spirits, I even compared her to myself, and I won, with
characteristic Dutch snobbery, because I came from a better
family, had more to offer, more intelligence...or I had to
drop out of the race because I was "stiff," "dull," and
"colourless." What did Erica look for in a girl friend, I wondered. Why did she want to live with me if her preference
was so clearly for loud, vulgar, superficial creatures like
Judy and Dolly? Those were two of a kind!

I hastened back with an old jug full of coffee from the
friendly grocery woman, and warmed my cold hands on it
along the way. Perhaps the kindness of the simple village
people would make up for a lot. With that thought the
world looked a little more rose-hued.

Then came the insight, problematic in itself but yet
optimistic in the present context, that Erica had invited a
moving-day guest to serve as a kind of lightning conductor.
She had felt sure the day would pass more easily with a
third person present. Was Erica then afraid to be alone with
me? In spite of the stubbornness she had shown with the
moving plan, perhaps she had already realized that I was
right, that it was madness to take this step and that she
should not have subjected me to it. In the following few
weeks she showed no sign of feeling this way, but in the long
run I was proved right: Erica couldn't stand it out there.

I had hardly settled into the modern room with its wide

windows overlooking the sea, which Erica had immediately assigned to me; I had just become resigned to the early rising and the commuting, and reconciled myself with the evenings that were as monotonous as the sound of the waves we heard endlessly; I had just ventured to tell Erica how contented I was—when her restlessness announced new dissatisfaction.

So we started going out in the evenings again, talked with the fishermen at the corner, had a drink in the café, as the populace watched us suspiciously, struck up acquaintances with the women in the stores, and went to visit a young painter Erica had met on the train. Then too there were bus trips to the movie in Alkmaar. Finally there came a week when we used the apartment only for sleeping: a frantic series of train and bus trips between Amsterdam and Egmond, with five hours of sleep in our dusty, neglected home.

At breakfast on Monday, I announced that I intended to come straight back to Egmond every night that week, and stay there. Erica duly took note of this, and went out by herself. She evidently enjoyed herself better without me, and when I thought I had shaken off the thought of her in the dimly lighted village or in the Alkmaar movie, or in Amsterdam with Dolly (who, by the way, had apparently gone out of our lives after the moving day), I enjoyed a few quiet weeks in my cosy room with books, knitting, and housekeeping. Sometimes I even took a walk at dusk along the sea, with a sandwich or fruit in my pocket if I should get hungry. Then I would eat my supper after dark. I was fairly happy. Especially I enjoyed the weekends, which I then spent more or less alone. I began to look better. I felt rested and had regained a little zest for living. I had also taken on the role of housekeeper, and did our shopping as soon as I

got out of the bus, kept the apartment in order and washed
and ironed our clothes. Yes, Erica's too, as I was accustomed
to do by then—although in spite of my efforts she looked
like an ill-groomed boy. We hardly saw each other; even in
the mornings I no longer waited for her. Before the bus left
I would speculate whether she could still catch it, and
watched for her half-amused. In those days she missed the
rattling monster most of the time, as well as the train connection in Castricum.

In the back of my mind I was aware of a vague pity, but
it was not strong enough to worry about—or rather, I did
not let myself be concerned. I simply did not want to think
of it consciously.

One night while I was reading in bed, I heard her come
home. It was earlier than usual. Generally I was already
asleep and did not even wake as her footsteps passed my
door. This time she stumbled around a little, waiting as it
were for my greeting. Then she knocked and asked if I was
asleep. When I said no—and how I have since cursed that
"no"!—she came in. By the light of my reading lamp I saw
that her face was puffy white, that she had rings under her
eyes. Even her strong constitution seemed unable to stand
the restless living of recent weeks.

"Oof, it's hot here!" she began, and took off her sweater.

"Central heating," I said in the tone we had used in the
beginning to show our respect for the modern installation
in the new building. I saw that she was wearing a dirty
blouse, although I had ironed until late the night before,
and had put in her closet a clean pile of the boy's shirts she
invariably wore. She looked dishevelled, as though she
hadn't taken off her clothes for days.

She sat down on the end of my bed and looked straight
at me, one eye half-closed in the smoke from her cigarette.

"I come with the pipe of peace," she said in mock seriousness, and took the cigarette between thumb and forefinger and held it between us at eye level.

Many answers flashed through my mind but all seemed inadequate or open to wrong interpretations. So I only smiled, though I would rather have said something. We sat like that for a while, I leaning against the pillows, Erica motionless, looking steadily at me. It has always been like that. Whatever happened, Erica never showed fear—I mean, the embarrassment that comes from shame and guilt. Whenever she decided to put her cards on the table, in order to end a conflict or to admit her mistakes, she did it without inner difficulty. Now I know that at those moments she had already settled the issue for herself. Confronting me was just an epilogue. After all she only had to justify her actions to herself.

"Next month I'm on the night shift again, and I talked to Betsie," she said finally. "She wants two weeks to look for another apartment and then we can move back in. We pay her moving expenses."

"You're crazy...you're completely mad!" They were the only words I could find. It was unbelievable. Was she really not quite right in the head? How had she found the insolent courage to ask Betsie, an office acquaintance of mine to whom we had sublet the Amsterdam apartment, to make room for us again after barely two months? And Betsie was no pushover; she was a rather aggressive woman in her forties who had shown considerable firmness and businesslike character in the first transaction, and had even insisted on a sublease contract. Now, as if it were the most ordinary thing in the world, Erica had persuaded her to pack her bags because we wanted to come back. Another victim of her whims had yielded. As for me, I simply didn't count.

The rage that flared up in me was so violent I could no longer lie down. I flung off the blankets and snatched my dressing gown from the bedside chair. But Erica was quicker than I. She covered me again, and bent over me with her hands on my chest, forcing me back. I saw her laughing face above me, smelled the familiar mixture of lavender soap and cigarette smoke she always carried with her and that I had always liked so much. But now it was repugnant to me, and the pressure of her strong hands took me outside of myself. I kicked her away with drawn-up knees and shouted uncontrolled curses and insults.

Immediately she let go of me and sat again at the foot of the bed. The outburst had somehow calmed me, and I lay against the pillows, a little ashamed of my temper.

"You push people to the edge of a precipice," I said, as if I had prepared the sentence in advance. "You do just as you like, and I don't matter."

At first Erica did not reply. She studied her fingernails, and I could not see her face. Suddenly she threw herself across the bed with her face in the blankets and lay motionless. It lasted an eternity. I didn't know what to do. Then I felt her hands around my hips and her head at my waist.

"Bea," she said haltingly, "Bea, don't you understand?"

The tears came only later, in an explosion of rage, hate, and disappointment. She reproached me for misleading her, for driving her to a confession, for letting her proceed in order to humiliate her later with my rejection. From my side there was nothing to say. How innocent, how blind and stupid I had been! I thought of Bas, of his accusation to Erica on his last visit. Ostensibly to save myself from the chaos of my thoughts—no, of my existence at that moment—I concentrated my emotions on Erica. Poor mixed-up Erica. But I could not touch her, comfort her.

Never again, I thought with revulsion. Yet was it revulsion? Was it not fear that, in spite of what had happened, I didn't feel revulsion for her? For even at that moment I realized that I had not indeed stopped her advances immediately; that I had, as she said, let her proceed. My feeling went out to her, I felt her humiliation with her, and I would have loved to comfort her, as she stood there kicking against the leg of the chair sobbing in powerless misery, by putting my hands on that shiny boy's head.

"That's the way I am!" she shouted at me then, "That's how I am!" Her face, wet with tears and distorted in an expression of pain and triumph at the same time, was turned to me. "And you are that way too! You, too, Bea! You might as well admit it! Admit it! Admit it!"

Sobbing wildly, but triumphantly like a world-conqueror, she kept repeating the phrase. And I fled, my whole body trembling, out of bed and—in retrospect it seems so ridiculous—into the kitchen, the only shelter I could reach.

Hours later we found each other again in my room, our faces calm, averted. Erica talked until daylight. It was not a plea; why should she defend herself? It was clear that she suffered more that night from what I then called (with a superiority feeling born of self-preservation and compassion) "Abnormality," than during the weeks when she first discovered she was "wrong." Wrong, she called it that night. It was the catharsis by which she then hoped to reconcile herself with "being wrong." She never used that expression again afterwards. Indeed she resigned herself to a nature that could not be changed, accepted the consequences, and enjoyed life. I have always admired that.

But that night I stood before the window with my back to her. How could I ever again confront her freely? I stared blindly at the moonlit sea, and saw nothing but the scenes of

Erica's unhappy childhood. Her experiences of the past year, of which I had suspected little or nothing, she depicted so clearly that, as it were, I underwent them myself. True power of observation was lacking until I suddenly became aware of the morning haze on the water and the gray deserted beach. Now I knew everything. But what purpose had it all served? Erica's confession and her accusation had driven us apart irrevocably, I then thought. Each must go her own way; living together was impossible.

But it was less than a month later that I came to the inescapable conclusion that we were tied to each other for life; that the short year with her had been, at least for me, decisive. I could no longer live without her; with her I could have only the strange existence that her miserable childhood had predetermined for her, and in which I could only be the spectator.

Chapter Eight

THE following month I was alone in Egmond, more alone than I had ever been before. Erica had packed a suitcase after that night, and gone—where, I did not know. When the door had closed behind her, I took a bath, scrubbed away the touch of those imperious hands and that insistent mouth; washed away the lavender-and-cigarette scent that lingered on my skin. I put clean sheets on the bed; then I took the train to Amsterdam. But when I got out at Central Station I realized that the whole world had changed, that I could not go back to the office.

I had always been a conscientious person, and even then I tried to convince myself that I had to go back to my job, that everyday work would help me more than doing nothing. But I couldn't do it. Somehow I forced myself to take a streetcar; but I had to get out halfway. I found myself in the neighbourhood of the Rijksmuseum and I went in.

What is it people do to themselves? Who can understand why I had to make those bitter hours even more bitter? Was I seeking an even deeper misery? I didn't know then and I still don't know. At that early hour in the museum I found only the usual copyists and a few ambitious tourists. Presently I came into a room where a group of young girls from the provinces, presumably under the guidance of their art teacher, were getting some firsthand views of the pictures they only knew from posters and calendars.

The little group offered diversion, and I clung to it. The fits of giggling and whispering had begun at daybreak, I suppose, in the Lodging for Christian Women. After stifled explosions of laughter at breakfast or lunch, brought on by a comical waiter or a nasty waitress, they had been temporarily controlled by a stern lecture from the teacher. Now things had got out of hand again; everything seemed to them strange and ridiculous, and their excitement had to find an outlet. Even Rembrandt's masterpieces, suddenly strange in spite of the familiar calendar reproduction, gave rise to choking attacks of laughter. It was an echo of my own school trips to Amsterdam.

And Erica? I knew about that period in her life too, since the night before. She had not laughed, of course. Her breathless fervour had found another focus—the still-young woman principal of her school who that year had unexpectedly assumed the task of leading the school trip. Erica stood next to her, furious at the childish behaviour of the others, her attention riveted with the complete absorption born only of love. She was a rather serious, unfeminine girl, for whom the school had always been a refuge, and where she had for the moment found the love she had missed. There she was safe, at least for most of the day, from the egoism, the ill-will, and the hysteria of her mother—a mother in name only, to whose ruthless domination she had been abandoned after her father had run away.

Things are strangely ordered in the world. The relationship between Erica and her parents was a bitter farce, a lugubrious joke of fate. It was especially so during the time before her father left, when he could only bear living with his wife as long as he could escape to the bar on the corner. At that time there had not even been the relief the school offered. She had stayed home, engulfed by the snarling, hate-laden voices—or had been taken in the middle of the night to Grandma's, because her home had become too dangerous for her.

"Yet I was glad when Ma came to get me," Erica had said the night before. "I thought Grandma was awful, though she did take good care of me. Can you understand that, Bea? Children are peculiar. I still preferred to be at home."

The rest of the day I wandered through the city, thinking of Erica, finding an escape in the incidents of her childhood and her adolescence. Again and again, in spite of all I could do to repress those images, I relived the moments before Erica's outburst, when I had been unresisting and she had taken me in her arms. Why had I not struggled, made it immediately clear to her that I did not want that love? Why had I not jumped out of bed at once? Every time that thought recurred, I looked for refuge in the stories she had told me afterwards. Later I would be able to interpret my reactions; now I couldn't, now I didn't want to.

At five-thirty I found myself in front of the newspaper office where Erica worked. From across the street I stared up at the modern facade, the inexorable wall of milk-glass behind which I knew Erica worked. I had stood in Paris like this, across the street from the hotel. Was I to count the milestones in my life this way? With what little will-power I had left I tore myself away from that spot and ran to the station. I fled and hid in Egmond. I sent a letter of resignation to the office "for reasons of health."

In the middle of that month, I slept a few times with the young painter Erica had met on the train, and whom I had subsequently encountered on one of my walks along the beach. It was a ridiculous business; all I remember of it is that I hoped that way to regain my balance.

After three weeks, I had to face the necessity of earning money. I tried to force myself to think constructively. I answered ads, and soon I found myself having to follow up my letters with interviews in Amsterdam. I was hired by an accountant's office, and ironically, the job paid more than I had earned before. It was a small firm in Amsterdam-South, and so I could avoid the centre of the city, and Erica. For the time being, I was able to control my desire to see her again. My life was a routine of travelling and working, travelling and sleeping. I was alone, and I told myself I preferred it that way.

Shortly before Christmas, I took a later train one night in order to buy some delicacies for a party that had been organized by the people in my new office. It was no coincidence that at half-past five I was walking past the newspaper building. I didn't deceive myself; I was trusting fate would respect my weakness. As it happened, I did not meet Erica there, but only a half hour later in the *Kalverstraat*, where she was wheeling her bicycle by the handlebar. I was struck by the fact that she was wearing a hat, a felt hat such as a man wears, with a pushed-in crown. Then I saw that in the shadow of its pulled-down brim one side of her face was swollen; her eye looked out from a green and purple bruise. And she limped a little. She tried a smile when she recognized me, but it seemed to hurt her. With an effort she pulled her face into a comical grin.

"What happened to you?" I asked. Her accident made the meeting easy for me. She looked at me significantly and again gave me that quasi-gay grimace.

"Dolly is a little sadistic by nature," she said.

The intent to shock me, the flatness of her statement, sobered me. "Is that so?" I said, hoping it would sound sarcastic and neutral at the same time.

She put her free hand through my arm and turned me half around toward her. "Come and have a cup of tea with me," she said, commandingly but cordially. She pinched my arm. "No excuses. The last train doesn't leave for hours."

So she presumed that I had stayed in Egmond—or maybe she had informed herself of it.

We sat opposite each other in the tearoom, and Erica loudly and cheerfully ordered a plate of pastry for us.

"You always liked cream custard!" she said, and whisked an eclair onto my plate. "Or would you rather have a meat pie? Waitress!"

"No, this is fine."

Only then did my heart start to pound; only then the emotion broke through. To save myself, I felt I must escape. I looked at my watch. "I'd like to catch the seven o'clock train. I'm expecting visitors tonight."

"Don't be a fool," Erica said, "when are you coming home?"

Home! Did she mean the Prinsengracht...or with her, wherever she lived?

"Never," I said. In my desperate effort at firmness, the word came out so explosively that people at the next table turned to look.

Erica began to laugh. "Sssssh..." she said. "You don't have to shout it from the rooftops!" She ate her pastry with relish, but I noticed that she nervously tapped her other hand on the table. She avoided my eyes, and perspiration appeared on her forehead. Our meeting had upset her too.

"The heat here is unbearable," she said irritably, and while she arranged her coat on the chair behind her she went on. "Now is your chance. Dolly threw me down the stairs." She pointed to her eye. "That's the third time she has attacked me, and though I'm crazy about her, enough is enough."

I got ready to leave. I could no longer bear the vulgarity of her life, or the arrogance with which she told about it. I was dizzy and sickish and longed for fresh air. What had these weeks of our separation done to Erica?

When I stood up she seized my wrist, and that strong small hand forced me to sit down again. Her face was chalk-white now, and the contrast with her blackened eye was startling.

"Admit, it Bea!" she said, "You might as well admit it!" They were the same words, but this time there was no triumph, no vehemence in her voice. I knew I would give in to her insistence, to the supplication in the face she now turned up to me, to the tearful eyes and the trembling mouth.

I pulled myself free and fled from the tearoom, out onto the street. I ran to the station. I couldn't control my wild sobbing.

That evening I wrote her a long letter. I had swallowed three bromide tablets so as not to get emotional. I would tell her in sober terms that I belonged in another world than hers. Paper is obliging, as they used to tell me in my child-hood. The written pages (which I let fly in pieces from the train window the next morning) gave me relief. But I had done no more than rinse off the bubbling, foaming surface; I did not dare disturb anything in the mysterious volcanic lake. I bought peace of mind by sidestepping the real issue.

Because of my resistance—which I could not define myself, but which sprang from my determination that Erica and I inhabited different worlds—she never dared to try to squeeze my true feelings from me. She understood that I had set up the barrier, that I had my right of asylum behind my boundary, inside the barbed-wire enclosure I had built for myself. She took the consequences and accepted my decision.

Once more I was to "confess to the devil." But after this mishap I was to be cured for good.

Our reconciliation came because of the war tension, which finally also penetrated my self-imposed isolation. I began to be worried about Erica's safety. First of all, I thought, she is half-Jewish. The office conversations helped me to see through the megalomania of many Dutch Jews, who found in patriotism a protection from their fears of Hitler's racial psychosis. The accountant was Jewish, and so were his clients for the most part. The bookkeeper and I were the only Christians among the personnel.

My environment enlarged my insight. It goes without saying that Erica, as the focus of my thoughts, became the centre of this new vision. I thought too of Van der Lelie, whose tactics I had feared since that first night of Erica's confessions. I had heard from my boss what his political attitude was. My boss spoke plainly; he subscribed to the paper only in order to be informed about Nazi sentiments among the Dutch—for one could read volumes between the lines.

Just as when Erica stayed away in France, I began to be tormented by worry and fear about her. This time the worry was no pretext for desire. My concern was stronger than self-interest. I wrote a note to her at the paper. Reading it through, it seemed exaggerated: What are your plans? Are you conscious of the danger? I tore it up and wrote another in which I asked to see her "for special reasons." She telephoned me at the office and suggested a café. Remembering our last meeting, I invited her to Egmond for the next Saturday afternoon. This was not what I intended, but when I heard the familiar, rather arrogant voice I had a vision of another scene in public, and asked her to my home. We were to meet in the Central Station at one-thirty.

That Saturday I waited an hour for her at the station; then I waited for more hours at home. She came toward supper time. I was so enervated from waiting; with alternating moods of indignation, doubt, disgust and regret, that the speech I had so carefully prepared degenerated into an accusation: Was she really waiting quietly for the German invasion? Was she completely unable to face reality? Did she think, by any chance, that the Nazis would make a detour and spare Holland?

Did she really suppose that Dutch Jews (or half-Jews— what was the difference?) would be treated any differently from those in Poland and Germany? Didn't she know that the director of her newspaper was known as a Nationalist Socialist? That Mr. Van der Lelie was hand in glove with their director? Was she such a fool as to count on him for protection? No, in her place I would pack my bags. Even more important people than she had already left the country!

Erica seemed extremely flattered by my anxious lecture. She hung on my words, and her eyes showed barely concealed amusement, and victory. It dawned on me then that Erica knew at last what went on inside me. And then I knew myself, too. Now I could no longer turn back, and when she put her arms around me and pressed me tightly to her, I did not resist. We stood like that a long time, until she whispered something in my ear. I did not understand her and she had to repeat it. Those few words she never spoke again; it was not necessary. We both knew they were irrevocable, and for ever. We accepted them, each in her own way.

When Erica had left on the last bus, I walked slowly home. It was now up to me to get her out of the country. The most obvious means were impossible; Erica had only the hundred guilders in her savings account, which I was still keeping for her. I had not been able to put aside much since I started my new job. In the next few days I was to face the same realities over and over again. There were two possibilities left, and I didn't know which of them I disliked most, Pa or Judy. And I did not conceal from myself that a loan from Erica's father would likely lead to a reunion with Judy. She would have to send the papers for Erica's emigration.

We had decided on America. It made no sense to stay in Europe, and Erica did not like the idea of the Dutch Indies. Judy...yes, Judy attracted her to the other side. Her name had not been mentioned during our discussion, but I was as aware of it as if Erica had shared her unspoken hope with me. She had avoided my eyes when I first mentioned the United States as the best solution, and she had reacted to it with *too much* indifference. Besides, we did not know anyone else who could send an affidavit. We both realized that, without mentioning it. And so, what? Erica would leave, I would stay behind. In those days of incessant worrying, of weighing the pros and cons, I would find myself sometimes at a dead end, where I would decide there was no way my plan could work. Erica would just have to stay here; we'd have to risk it. Thousands of others, after all, were in the same position and couldn't leave either. Perhaps the impending danger would be averted. And if things did get worse, we could always plan an escape later. But I had lost faith in my own sincerity; no, I couldn't even give my hidden feelings a chance. And hastily I stepped back into the pattern of my plan.

The proposition was highly amusing to Erica. "Pa!" she exclaimed when I told her. She started to giggle, repeating his name in every pitch. But finally she made a decision; she slapped her knee and said, "Okay, go ahead. Why not, after all?"

I awaited the outcome of the interview in a café across from the newspaper building. She was back within the time I had expected her to take, and I saw at once that she had received more than a simple refusal. Without speaking, she sank down in a chair beside mine.

"Well?" I asked, but she did not answer.

After what seemed an endless silence, she said with a tortured smile, "You know, Bea, Dolly and I went to a fortune teller the other day."

When she saw that I was surprised and a little irritated, she went on quickly, "Well, for fun, of course, in a silly mood, although Dolly...anyway, the creature told me I was very musical, and that I should study the violin." She smiled with sarcasm. "Only now I understand. You may as well know, Bea, that my father was a Polish violinist."

She said no more, and after a look at her face I called the waiter and led her out of the café as quickly as possible. On the street, I put an arm around her shoulders. As we walked along slowly I waited for an explanation. Now and then I squeezed her shoulder encouragingly, and when I said "Tell me quietly" and got no response, I let it go at that. Finally I grew tired of the aimless wandering, and decided to force the matter. As casually as possible I said, "So your father was a Polish violinist."

I had struck the right tone. It sounded so matter-of-fact, and therefore so ridiculous, that suddenly we both laughed—Erica nervously and uncontrollably. Then the whole story came out. Erica's request for a loan had been flatly refused by Pa. She had insisted, pointing out that after all she was his daughter, and that he had done nothing for her since he had left her mother.

He did have to admit that she had never asked him for anything before. But he flew into a rage and, while the office personnel in the next room cocked their ears, told her bluntly that she was not his daughter. He spared no details, and depicted her mother—"that whore"—in full. Erica fled, and, since she had to pass through the outer office on her way out, had the whole office staring at her. Erica put great emphasis on that last detail.

"What kind of business is he in?" I asked to divert her.

"Pa is..." she broke off, for the word "Pa" was now out of place. "He is an importer."

"I still think 'Pa' is a good name," I said, "You've always used it in a mocking way."

"All right then—'Pa'," she consented. She put her arm through mine and we began walking at a brisk pace. For the moment I had helped her, but when we parted after dinner and I watched her go, I saw by her bent head and her posture that she had by no means recovered from the blow.

After a sleepless night during which I completely identified myself with Erica, I called early at the newspaper. She wasn't there, and nobody had heard from her. Then I tried to trace her, which was ridiculous, because I didn't know Dolly's last name.

For two weeks I waited for word from her. Often I phoned the paper, but they had had no news either. At last I even asked to speak to Van der Lelie, who did not come to the phone, but passed word to me that Miss Boekman was no longer considered a member of the staff.

Chapter Nine

I<small>N</small> the end, it was Dolly—no less—who phoned. She did not seem so haughty as she was the one time I had met her. "Could you come right away?" she asked. "I can't handle her any more, and she's going to pieces."

I made excuses at the office and hurried to the address, on an ancient canal in the old and run down part of town. It was one of those dilapidated houses which should have been declared uninhabitable, but that, as long as it escaped the notice of the housing commission (or didn't give up the struggle and collapse of its own weight), would have a certain attraction for people artistically inclined and rather insecure themselves. Real, hardworking artists, I reflected with the pedantry that supported my self-confidence, would live in solid buildings where work can go on without the daily intrusion of wear and decay. I could almost have spanned the facade with my outstretched arms and set the small building straight.

At the top of the hollow-worn steps I looked in vain for a nameplate, and since my ringing brought no answer and the door stood ajar, I presumed I was to go in. The small hall was dark and chilly. Dolly had said I was to go to the top floor, and I finally made it with the help of my sense of touch. I heard a waltz played on a piano, and the tapping of feet.

Since I didn't know what else to do, I called out, "Dolly!" which made me feel silly, but the waltz was interrupted and a man's voice yelled, "Dolly, there's someone in the hall!" The door was opened by a girl in a bathing suit. I entered a

long empty room, a kind of studio, with mirrors and a bar
along one of the walls; a bed, a piano, a little chest, and a
trapeze in the corners. At the piano sat a young man who
turned to look at me indifferently for a moment, and in the
middle of the room stood a few girls who stared curiously.

Dolly came up immediately. So she was a dancer. I had
never inquired about her profession, but now it seemed logical. I did not know anything about dancers, and I must
confess that at the time I looked down on them. Or, more
accurately, I was suspicious of anyone whose ambition was
to jump around on a stage and twist her body into all sorts
of contortions. Dolly's shabby training suit, which exposed
her unnaturally long and muscular legs to the top of her
thighs, did not put me at ease.

A little at a loss, I looked up at her, into the hard blue
eyes at the translucently white face, the high smooth brow
which concealed the alien, puzzling thoughts I could not
guess. With an impatient gesture she pushed a lock of damp
red hair behind her ear. What could I say? What did she
expect of me? But she had already gone to a door at the end
of the room, and she spoke in a tone one might apply to a
sick dog: "She's in there."

The little room, which I concluded was Erica's sanctuary,
was dark, indescribably dirty and neglected; I saw that in one
glance. The door closed behind me, and at Dolly's command
the waltz and the thumping resumed. Erica lay on a low wide
couch under the window, her face in a pillow. The covers
had slid partly off, and I saw that she was fully dressed.

How can I describe the rest of that afternoon? The
washing and scrubbing, the tidying up that I started feverishly when it dawned on me that Erica was sleeping off a
drunk...the revolting details that revealed to me the kind of
life she was leading now...her hat and coat in the vomit on

the floor; plates and glasses, covered with a layer of mould
in the washbasin; the grimy clothes, empty bottles, over-
flowing ashtrays, old newspapers, spoiled food. I did not
know a human being could get into such a state. And as I
kept working stubbornly and grimly, the lessons in the studio went on. Erica had suffered her despair and desolation
with the rhythm of the dancing feet and the beat of the
music in her ears. Within an easy calling range there had
been people. But she had made no appeal, and no help had
been offered.

I took advantage of an intermission between two lessons
to empty the scrub bucket. It humiliated me to ask Dolly
where to go, to let her know what I was doing. Under her
indifferent eyes I felt an overzealous Florence Nightingale,
a grotesque saint. I asked her for clean bed linen; she didn't
have any at the moment, and besides, what for? Tomorrow
it would be the same thing again. There was no criticism, no
scorn in her eyes; she only shrugged her shoulders. So I ran
out of the house and in a store nearby I bought bed linen,
towels, underwear, and a pair of pyjamas.

Erica did not even wake up when I rolled her over as I
washed her. I washed carefully because of the many bruises,
and pulled the pyjamas over her limp body.

"Dolly is a little sadistic by nature..."—those words kept
repeating themselves in my head.

By the time I had finished cleaning and hung up her
hat and coat, it was evening. The lessons were over and
Dolly had gone out. Once more I went outside and got coffee, bread, butter, and cheese. In the filthy little kitchen I
made my own evening meal. When toward eleven o'clock
Erica finally awoke from her heavy sleep, I stood by her bed
with a cup of coffee and a few aspirins. She greeted me with
an enigmatic smile, and after she had looked around the

room she spoke with the mockery I had feared before: "Hello, Florence Nightingale."

I stayed with her that night. In the morning she permitted herself to be taken, silent and unresisting, to Egmond. During the train ride she made only one remark. With that eternal derision in her voice and on her face—and wasn't that really self-hatred?—she said, "At least Dolly saved the expense of a cleaning woman."

I turned my head to the window, but from the corner of my eye I could see that she quickly blinked away the welling tears.

Under my care (as unobtrusive as I could make it) she recovered visibly. I knew from experience that her recovery would be the beginning of a new phase in her life. Her birthright had been denied, but I could see that she would graft a new branch over the wound she had suffered, and would nourish it into full bloom, to hide the scar at least temporarily. She started to talk confidently about America, and I, who had seen the worry and concern of Jewish colleagues at the office, strengthened her in the decision.

My boss had dropped a small bombshell among the office personnel by calling us all together one morning and announcing that he had sold the business and was leaving for America. I noticed some embarrassment behind his words. As a well-to-do Jew who had the money for an escape, he felt guilty and even a little ashamed for those who were exposed to the same danger as he, but had no way of getting away from it. Also, of course, he felt more Dutch than Jewish, and his course of action, which I thought sensible, made him feel like a deserter. He sought to justify himself by pointing out the danger once again. He made quite a speech. First he summarized the political situation, then he reviewed the machinations of the Dutch

National Socialists and their position in regard to Germany. He finished by stating that the same fate would come to Dutch Jews as to those in the Third Reich. He took a book from his desk and passed it to the bookkeeper to be circulated among us. After a time my turn to read it came. It pictured the misery of the Jews under the Nazi regime, with endless details and statistics. According to the racial theory Erica would be stamped a Bastard-Jew I, and her fate would be little different from that of the "real" Jews.

Beside the extra stir caused by the sale of the firm and the impending departure of the director, the atmosphere at the office was oppressive. Ceaseless arguments and discussions among the personnel interrupted the work. One thought the boss was a coward and a traitor; another envied him and despised him for the same reasons. Nobody admired him for his insight. Though their peace of mind was disturbed, they could not admit he was right, and so surrender the security that being Dutch first, and Jewish second, gave them.

I took the book home with me one night for Erica to see. She tried to hide her feeling of revulsion by pretended casualness. But the remark she made cut straight through my soul.

"Ridiculous, Bea! Now I'm suddenly a Jewess!" She shook her head in disbelief and half-amused despair. "It's all in a lifetime." She mimicked her grandmother's favourite expression. "America, America, here I come!" she added with a comical overtone. Yet I was sure that she only considered leaving because her personal difficulties had forced her to seek a change.

Before the end of the week, we composed a letter to Judy, which was to be signed by me. "It's always better if someone else asks," was the way Erica put it.

Before I signed, something suddenly occurred to me. "Perhaps your real father wasn't a Jew at all! " It was out before I knew it. We had not touched on the subject again, and I was startled at my own *faux pas*. But of course the thought was important, and it had to be expressed.

"Then you'll have to ask Ma about that," she said without hesitation.

"I?"

"Yes, of course; who else? It's your idea—and you don't think I ever want to see her again, do you?"

"But I simply can't...How can I ask her, Erica? That's impossible. I'm an outsider. She'd throw me out..."

But the idea of calling Ma to account for her sin had taken hold. Erica was not to be dissuaded, and I resigned myself with reluctance.

The conversation with Ma in the General's elegantly furnished living room might as well have been recorded. I can still repeat it word for word, and the pain I felt is still sharp. First there was the hearty reception: "Dearie" this, "Dearie" that...and the diminishing of cordiality when my nervousness made it plain that I was not there on a courtesy call. Then came my long-winded, stammering introduction to the subject, and the enormous question that would not let itself be disguised in vague terms.

Her reply was an impassioned monologue, with a dramatic description of her circumstances in those years—the plea of the condemned. The role of accuser suited me badly. I almost felt guilty myself at her passionate defense, as she wrung her hands, then employed them in a gesture to her heart, then stretched them out to me in despair. The "*He*" this and "*He*" that—meaning her lawful husband—would have stayed the hand of an executioner. But I had not come to administer justice, and I tried to explain this to her. She did not even hear me with my repeated, "But Ma, all that is none of my business; I just wanted..."

Finally her materialism had the last word. "And why do you think then that I gave the child my money, the only few pennies that have ever been tossed in my lap. Those three thousand guilders, I inherited them from Jan—that was her father—"she interrupted herself, "he had died and left them to me." She burst into sobs. "I had never seen him again, but he didn't forget me!"

So the secret of the inheritance was solved: it wasn't an uncle who had willed her the three thousand guilders, but her lover! Erica had been right in suspecting there was something odd about the money. I remembered only too well her strange behaviour after she received it. She had hinted at it, too, during the night of confession; penance money, she called it. She had referred to the money when she told of the repeated extramarital adventures of her mother, and described the misery of her adolescence. Those affairs had taken place under Erica's nose; in puberty the child guessed much but knew nothing until one night she needed her mother and found that she was not alone in bed.

Erica had been sent to a convent school to "get her out of the way," as she called it, and to "get absolution for Ma." Already, while Erica told me, I had sympathised with the dismay of the sixteen-year-old girl who had discovered her mother's love-life, and had been "dragged" from the "glorious" girls' high school and "locked up—bang!" in the religious, "abnormal" atmosphere of the convent.

Hearing it again, my compassion for Ma changed to horror. I got up and prepared to leave. Ma began powdering her nose. An oppressive silence hung over us; we avoided looking at each other. With one hand on the doorknob, I spoke, and it struck me how cold and cruel my voice sounded.

"I only came to ask whether her father was Jewish."

Ma turned to me in a rage, her face blotched with crying. She squinted her eyes venomously. "If she's so anxious to save her skin, she'd better ask that bastard too!" She laughed sneeringly. "That is, if he knows! He always used to do all he could to find out what went on. And he gave me his word, too, the sneaky coward, that Erica would never...The dirty traitor! You could expect something like that of a Jew! Hitler is right!"

I didn't wait for the rest. At the front door I could still hear her voice.

My head was spinning. In the sober light of midday, in the well-to-do, friendly atmosphere of the It Straat where the first green of spring was already appearing on the trees, and the lawns were being prepared by the city gardeners, my visit seemed improbable. I shook my head to wake from the bad dream, and my thoughts fastened themselves to a memory that emerged perhaps to orientate me, to restore to me the identity of the Bea of years ago, the original I. It may also have come because I realized that now Erica had taken leave of her mother through me.

It was the day of my mother's funeral, together with the lifeless body of the little boy that had caused her death. In the nursery, with the flowered pattern of the closed curtains lighted so strangely by the daylight, I stood peeking out at the black coach and the carriage down in the street. The maid, to whose care I had been entrusted, had forgotten me; she sat crying with her face in her hands. I was too young to understand what was going on, and was innocently curious at the commotion downstairs in front of the gate.

The door of the room opened, and my father and my grandparents came in quickly. I was lifted up and overwhelmed with kisses and caresses. For the first time—and never again during my childhood—I tasted the salt of grown-up tears. For a few minutes the little girl had been drawn within the family; the adults were looking for her. Small as she was, they needed her in the family circle before the slow journey to the cemetery began.

And seeing her, the grandmother realized that she was needed more at home than on the last trip with her daughter. She had made an unbelievably heavy sacrifice, and played with me until the black carriages returned to the door. The memory of a memory: it has stayed with me all those years. Only then at twenty-eight could I understand what my grandmother experienced in those hours when, pretending to be cheerful, she helped dress and undress the dolls, and entered into the imaginary world of the little girl who, with natural mimicry hugged and admonished her porcelain friends in the voice and intonation of her mother. She had had to listen to that—while her daughter was being buried.

Memories of my early life are few. Nothing remains of the years from my mother's death to my entering high school. Only the other day I had to calculate carefully when someone here in America asked me how old I was when my mother died. By her death, a vacuum was created in my childhood. Nevertheless I preserved an image of my mother that with the help of my father's reminiscences grew to heavenly stature.

How different it had been with Erica! A mother of flesh and blood, it is true, instead of my own guardian angel, but one who took out her disappointment and guilt feelings on her child. At exactly two o'clock, the operator announced a call from Egmond. It was Erica, as we had agreed.

"And...? What did she say?" she asked, her voice tense.

"It was no use." I had to be discreet for I didn't know whether the line was clear. "She didn't want to tell. You should ask *him*."

"Oh yes?" There was menace in Erica's voice, then silence.

"Are you still there?"

"Yes." And again nothing but the humming and crackling of the connection. But also the hatred, the hate more violent because it was powerless, brewing behind the silence, a hate I could almost literally hear.

"See you later," she finally said drily, and the connection was broken.

I went home that night with fear and apprehension, but Erica asked no further questions. In two words she thanked me for my trouble. To tell the truth, I was glad not to have to relate the conversation with Ma.

After dinner Erica took out the letter to Judy and asked me to sign it. Together we took it to the mailbox. Before I let it go through the slot, I looked questioningly at Erica.

"Go ahead, Miss Milquetoast!" she said.

After that there was the waiting for a reply. Already a week later, it was my first question when I came home at night. Soon Erica said she couldn't stand it any more and asked me to spare her. She'd let me know soon enough if a letter came. Meanwhile she ordered me to get information from the American consulate and the shipping company. She did nothing herself to prepare for her departure. During the next two weeks I would always find her at home, perhaps on the couch with one of the books I provided for her, with the phonograph playing or the radio on a Dutch station. Following those two weeks I often found the bird had flown. There would be a note in my room: "Have gone to the movies," or a "Have gone to Amsterdam." As time went on, there was less explanation: "Am not coming home tonight." And finally, no notes at all. She stayed away a great deal.

One morning when I brought her breakfast in bed (which I had begun to do when she needed it and kept on doing while she slept at home), she said, "I'd better put my cards on the table. You know everything now anyway. I'm in love again. A cellist in the women's orchestra in a beergarden. You ought to come and have a look at her; she's fantastic!"

Thus she made me a partner in her escapades, and at the same time she made it easy for me to be objective. Thus, quite naturally, we entered a new phase in our relationship.

That same afternoon after work, with an initiative unusual for me, I visited the café in the centre of the city where Erica had lost her heart. As I hesitated at the revolving door, trying to find my bearings, I asked myself how Erica had come to find this quasi-German café, with its deceiving atmosphere of coziness. I would never have gone near such a place; the patrons were from another planet. My helplessness was noticed by a waiter, and after I stammered a description of Erica, he surveyed me from head to toe with a sly smirk and winking toward another waiter directed me toward the platform. There I found Erica at a table, practically at the feet of the cellist. She was absorbed with her new flame, and she hardly looked up when I sat down beside her, my whole body in a state of perspiration. But the smile on her face was for me. Without turning her head she said, "How do you like her?"

"How do you like her?"—now that I knew her secret, she valued my judgment and sought my approval. I could scarcely tell her the truth: that I find a woman with a cello between her legs unattractive to begin with. When I used to go to concerts with my father, who was a great music lover like many middle-class Dutch, a programme was occasionally built around the performance of a woman cellist. I

never liked it. The lady invariably dressed for the occasion
in frills and décolleté to accentuate her fragility. She only
succeeded in making a greater contrast to the instrument
she held clumsily between her thighs, bringing me confusion and dismay instead of the enjoyment of an art. I argued
with my father about it afterward, but he thought my reaction was exaggerated.

Erica's new girl friend came off a little better; my artistic expectation was less in the beer-garden. Besides, she
seemed more energetic than consecrated, and she bowed
the instrument as if she were sawing kindling.

It was only a few days later, when Inge—that was her
name—visited us in Egmond and played for us, that I discovered she really possessed a remarkable talent and was an
artist to the tips of her fingers. In Erica's room, her head
bent over the instrument so the dark straight hour fell over
her cameo-pale face, she seemed different from the young
woman who had suggested the woodcutting simile to me in
the smokey restaurant. There she played for a living—a
concession that didn't seem to bother her, for she had
walled off her other self and kept it inviolate. In our home
she set it free; her playing was almost obsessed.

I liked her a lot and could understand Erica's passion
for her. It didn't even annoy me when she stayed overnight
once a week. Then I looked after her as I looked after Erica.
What did bother me in the beginning was the fact that Inge
was German. It was well known in those days that our
neighbours to the East did not get permission to travel outside the country, unless of course they performed espionage
service. One spoke then with the emphasis of double meaning about "German tourists," and although such suspicions
as these were dismissed as over-cautious by some people, I
did not ignore the possibility so easily. All artists came under

the surveillance of Goebbels' organization, that much I
knew for sure. Therefore the little orchestra in which Inge
played was making cultural propaganda for the Third
Reich, and perhaps the members also had orders that took
them beyond the four walls of the beer-garden.

My doubts were soon dissipated. Inge won our confidence by speaking freely about conditions in Germany. As
she began talking, the heart-shaped face distorted in resent-
ment and rage, she convinced us of her hatred for the
regime. One had no choice, she said; one had to live. Several
members of the ensemble were staunch Nazis, however,
and—she whispered with an involuntary look around and a
little shudder of her shoulders—they got paid more because
they did other work. She did not suggest what those other
jobs were, but it was clear enough. Her pale face whitened
even more as she warned us; things would go wrong.
Germany had her eye on Holland.

Erica began to whistle, and put on a record. I knew that
reaction. My heart beat suddenly in my throat. We were still
waiting for Judy's answer; if it were a "yes" and included the
necessary cash, then there would still be a question as to
whether Erica would leave. I had no illusions. At that
moment, Inge was more important to her than the desire
for change, even for self-preservation. And time was pressing. It was the beginning of April.

At the American consulate where I had gone secretly to
see if there might be a message for Erica, the Jews were
waiting in lines. The steamship company where I had
reserved passage for Erica just in case—would no longer be
put off with promises. I had already been thinking of ways
to borrow the money. It was up to me; Erica simply couldn't
be bothered.

But now, busy with the gramophone, she said suddenly,

"*Ich bin halb Jude.*" Then she turned quickly so Inge's reaction would not escape her. I was aware of the drama that played between them. The statement was not made in connection with the danger, but purely to find out how much the racial theory had influenced Inge, and whether her feelings for Erica were strong enough to survive it. In spite of myself, I felt sorry for Inge.

"That is impossible!" she said at first, and was ready to scold Erica for a bad joke. But Erica stared fixedly at her; she did not let her eyes go, and she betrayed nothing. Finally Inge turned helplessly to me. I still remember how uncomfortable I felt; I confirmed it with a nod.

"But then..." Inge began, "then..." She jumped up and looked wildly from Erica to me. She struggled for the right words to express her alarm. "But then there is no time to lose!" Her look attached itself to me with urgency. "What are you doing? What can we do?"

She sat down again. With a few steps, Erica was behind Inge's chair; she pressed her face against the other girl's. I got up and reached for the full ashtrays. As I went to empty them I heard Erica whispering in Inge's ear. She has stood the test, I thought with some bitterness. Always the test. Perhaps I had subconsciously hoped for a different kind of reaction from Inge. Who knows? Perhaps now I have grown too suspicious; maybe I am trying to dig too deep.

Soon after that first unaccountable bitterness, I came to the conclusion that Erica had reconciled herself with the circumstances of her illegitimacy. She had been recognized by Pa, and was registered as his daughter. Rather than calling Ma to account once more, or questioning Pa, she had resigned herself to the situation.

Chapter Ten

TOWARD the end of April, I gave up waiting. Judy was apparently a finished affair, and I reproached myself for not paying more attention to Erica's words: "For Judy those things are more for a thrill. She can take it or leave it." No wonder Erica didn't talk about it! She must be deeply hurt at Judy's desertion. Or else the whole thing left her cold. After all, except for Inge, there was nothing and nobody in the world. Erica's love-life dominated everything under the sun. It had been that way with Dolly and Judy; it was that way again. And I had to admit to myself that even I had once been the centre of her interest—albeit with less absorption.

I toiled on at the office and did overtime, as much as I was allowed, for which I was paid extra. We certainly needed the money; I was working for two now. Regularly Erica came to borrow from me, mumbling something about "we'll settle later." The remainder of Ma's "inheritance" was still in the savings bank. She didn't ask for it and I didn't dare mention it any more. We have both forgotten about it; as far as I know it's still there. Now and then I still come across the bankbook. It has always travelled among my papers; it is yellowed now.

At that time I was living alone again for the most part. Evenings I took work home with me. It was a diversion and a satisfaction to do the work my boss entrusted to me down to the last details before his departure. His appreciation warmed me in my brooding loneliness. Our farewell was cordial. He would not forget me: "The best secretary I'll ever have. If you ever need help..." At the time he didn't suspect any more than I did that he would have a chance to make good on this promise. For years now I have been his secretary in New York. It was to him I turned when I decided after the war that I wanted to leave Holland. But that's getting off the subject. The new director came to the office, and I got along well with him right away too. In an office I seem always to be at my best.

Resignedly I waited for what would come. The fatalism in the country amazed me, but assured me too. Perhaps everything would come out all right. Maybe I had let myself be carried away by my anxiety about Erica. Even at the office everyone was calmer since the boss had left. It was a relief not to be reminded of the danger any more. The subject for discussion now was the new owner of the business.

Once a week Erica and Inge spent the night at Egmond. I lived for those evenings, for then they admitted me into the sanctuary of their union. What Erica did in Amsterdam, I didn't know. She confided to me only that she spent the evenings at the beer-garden and then went with Inge to the rooming house. So night after night she sat at Inge's feet in the café! How could she stand it? The significant smile of that waiter came to my mind's eye. I shook myself like a wet dog.

Then came the blow—for Erica at least, and for me too in a certain sense, because I drew conclusions from it. The orchestra ended its engagement on May 4 and left for Germany. Erica stood before me that evening, unannounced. She was completely stunned.

"But didn't Inge know about it beforehand?" I asked in my innocence.

Erica shrugged her shoulders, crestfallen. "Of course, but she didn't want to say goodbye."

"Come on, now," I blurted out, "you don't believe that yourself!"

She said nothing, and disappeared into her room. But in the middle of the night she came and sat on my bed. She was still fully dressed, and so desperate she had to speak out. First she talked about Inge. In her misery she proffered confidences for which I had not asked, and which were painful to me.

"She knew about it," she said finally. "She'd known about it for a week. They were going to stay until the end of the month and then play in Rotterdam—that was the official plan. But last week she heard they were called back. They weren't allowed to talk about it. She didn't dare tell; it was a secret too dangerous to let leak out, even to me. She didn't trust any of the others. She was afraid my reaction might be too obvious."

"That speaks volumes," I said alarmed. "When the Germans call their people home..." I didn't finish the sentence. Erica fumbled in the pocket of her skirt, and drew out a wrinkled envelope and handed it to me. The letter had an American stamp, and was registered. I knew immediately who the sender was, and what the letter had meant.

"I've cheated you," she said superfluously. "She answered a week after we wrote. I spent the money."

Hundreds of times images from the period that followed have slid through my mind, and now after thirteen years they have fallen into place to make one complete picture. One inward glance is enough to make me feel it all again, to realize in spite of the wrenching pain at the loss of Erica that for six months I had been her only recourse, and in this way she belonged to me as much as I could let her.

What came afterward, the tormenting question as to why I had put those restrictions on our relationship, and my regret about that decision which I never doubted at the time, but which I was later unable to understand—that is my burden, my heritage of the whole episode. That heritage has settled in me like a tumour deep in a tissue, harmless so long as I was able to build new cells around it. Sometimes, on sleepless nights, that tumour takes on a life of its own, and then only my determination can save me, only willpower can press down the doubt and regret and seal them in again. After all, it can never be amended, never lived again! Externally I have finished with it all, the slate is clean, my life has gone on. But now that I call myself to account about that part of my life, which was the most important, the only part that mattered, that was decisive, let me also have the courage to look once more at the details of that composite picture of the first occupation months.

What strikes me first, then, is the shock at Erica's outrageous betrayal—which missed its full impact at the time because I also secretly experienced a strange and inexplicable satisfaction in it.

Then afterwards, before I had time to regain my balance, and while I was making a number of uncoordinated efforts to get Erica out of the country, the German invasion came. *Too late, too late!* was all I thought, for my first reaction centred around Erica alone. It was indeed characteristic of my state of mind that I was more distraught at Erica's precarious position than at the disaster that had fallen upon the country.

So well I remember how she sat near the radio hour after hour, first in a feverish tension, but soon in total dejection...a lonely vigil.

For me, the war began there in Erica's room. The image of Erica, bent over the apparatus—sucked into it, as it were—represented for me the invasion, the battles, the bombardments, the defeat of a proud people. I saw only Erica, so completely paralyzed, so crushed that the voice from the loudspeaker was her only support.

And I knew too, from an occasional dazed movement of her head, that in addition to her despair there was a growing wonder at her own reckless actions. It oppressed me to see her like that, but all the same I sensed in myself a righteousness, a shouldering wick of satisfaction that I watched uneasily and that was not extinguished even by my pity and fear.

I exaggerated my housekeeping because only physical activity gave me release from my torturing thoughts. Every time I returned from my job, or from shopping in the village where the people huddled together or passed each other with sad smiles, I found Erica just as I had left her. She had lost everything—work, money, relatives, friends—she had nothing and nobody left but me. Thus we started the occupation. Erica had burnt all her bridges behind her.

To call her back to reality, I spoke of Inge: where would she be? would we still hear from her? My intention was good, but Erica did not take it so. She silenced me with a wild shake of her head, as if my questions were too much for her, as if they evoked associations that would destroy her. I could have bitten off my tongue. Even now I wince when I think of that crude stupidity, that cruel mistake.

Yet I didn't dwell long on it. We had to make plans. Under the circumstances we were better off in Amsterdam. I foresaw that travelling back and forth through the occupied country would be too complicated in the long run. And who knew what lay in store? Better to leave the coast of our own accord than to be forcibly evacuated later with the other inhabitants. I was pessimistic from the start and yet, in retrospect, I acted from intuition. I then had no idea of the misery that was ahead of us.

I asked Erica to look for a place to live, for I had to go

back to the office myself. "But mind you—not in the old
city—no artistic slums," I warned.

She answered with a long, searching look, and said
sharply, "Madam imposes conditions. Madam is boss now!"
At that moment she saved us from a horrible relationship.
The position of supporter and guardian angel, which of
course I had had to take on, had gone to my head. Erica saw
through it immediately. Her proud resistance sobered me up
at once. So we could start on this existence through the abnormal time on a healthy basis. In spite of her dependence she
remained my equal, she gave me no chance to dominate. And
I can still feel shame for that momentary desire for power,
especially because I had to suppress an urge to dominate several times after that. I must say my position was anything but
easy. Erica's yearning for independence left little room for my
urge to protect her. Her self-sufficiency discouraged help.

She did not seem aware of obligations. The idea of
"mine and thine" had no importance for her. At this
moment I happened to be in a favourable position; if the
positions were reversed, would she not naturally accept
responsibility for me? It was only coincidence that such an
opportunity didn't present itself. That's the way Erica
looked at life, and it was that philosophy I had to struggle
with. It was up to me to keep the scales in balance.

In the summer months of 1940, Erica went her own
way again. She did feel the importance of the tie between
us; our top floor in one of the new districts of Amsterdam
did serve as home for her. She was warm and full of consideration for me, but still she remained independent. She
had no job and wasn't looking for one, yet she was busy. I
knew what she was doing as well as if she had told me herself, but I pretended ignorance. When she stayed away for
days at a time, I waited for her with fear in my heart. It

suited her character perfectly to be doing illegal things, to perform sabotage.

They were small acts, which were the beginning of organized resistance to the enemy. Then it still looked like child's play and the results were insignificant. For my part I made it easy for both of us by my silence, by playing naive. I kept busy at the office, and supported us both. But the conviction grew in me that Erica would not survive the war if she stayed in Holland. Apart from the persecution of the Jews, of which there was no sign at first—but which I waited for like the explosion of a time bomb—my insight into Erica's character gave me sufficient warning of danger from another direction. Yes, I thought, the risk from her actions is greater than the danger from her origin. She could not compromise or make the best of it; she couldn't stay out of the line of fire like the mass of the population. Her life was a promissory note. She had construed her right to existence out of bits and pieces; her future only seemed to ensure happiness when she challenged fate—fate, which was as familiar to her as an enemy in single combat.

I had to protect Erica against herself—that's how I saw it. Didn't I admire her for her initiative, her courage? Wasn't I proud of her? In a certain sense, of course; I don't have to admit otherwise. At the same time, I realized that heroines like Erica are doomed. They are too spontaneous, too unpredictable. With other people, the heart may start them off, and that's as it should be; but then reason takes over the job and determines the outcome and the success. I knew only too well that Erica's heart would continue to pipe the tune. So I made plans in secret. I bought a forged identity card with money I got from the jewellery my grandmother had left me. I waited for the right moment to persuade Erica to leave. Meanwhile I sabotaged her activi-

ties. Yes, I even kept her from her dangerous work by asking her to do time-consuming marketing. So she went out
and stood in line for hours, to contribute her part to the
household.

In the late summer, when Erica bluntly refused to try to
make an escape, and told me to save myself any trouble
along that line, I pretended to have a nervous breakdown,
and that way I kept her at my bedside for three weeks. I'm
not ashamed of it; I had only one purpose: to protect Erica.
And didn't I have a right to do that? The underground
movement could find someone else to take her place. Call
me egoistic, call me immoral, I don't care. Any means could
serve my purpose; I had no scruples.

In November we had a visit from Ma. Ma, the Nazi
Gefährtin!

I was home alone. The unexpected call put me in a
panic. If only she would disappear before Erica got home!
There was still an hour until dinner, but Erica might get it
into her head to be early. The odds were ten to one, but the
possibility was there.

I was absolutely rude, professing exaggerated surprise
at her visit. I did not ask her in, I pretended to be in a hurry,
said I was cooking supper, and finally told her Erica didn't
usually come home for dinner. It was no good. Ma followed
me to the kitchen and made herself comfortable on a stool.

She was wearing the uniform of the National Socialist
Women's Organization, and she looked grotesque in the
young-woman's suit and the little cap slanting across her
shoulder length black hair. Next to her rouged cheeks, her
lips looked blue, and the jet-black lines at her eyes accented
the pale yellow wrinkled skin.

But she exuded girlish spirits and she insisted on telling
me how her activity as a group leader had rejuvenated her,

and how her life had been enriched. She also tried to convince me of the importance of her position and her indispensability. I listened to all of it in silence, while aversion, pity and certain calculations played touch-and-go in my head.

But the desire to avoid a meeting between her and Erica won out. I found a final pretext: didn't she want to go and have a drink with me in a nice place around the corner. I had nothing in the house and I didn't like to see her without a drink. No use! Ma hadn't seen "the child" for so long, and she had chosen this hour to be sure to find her at home. The drink could wait.

"What the hell are you doing here?" was Erica's greeting when she stuck her head in the kitchen door at six-thirty.

"Now, now, sister..." Ma began. She got up and straightened the narrow skirt of her uniform. Like a fish out of water she gasped for her next words; Erica did not wait for them.

"All right, Ma, get out of here. There's nothing here for you any more." And with a sneer at Ma's outfit, "We don't receive National Socialists here." She held the door wide open and nodded her head toward the stairs.

It was clear that Ma was prepared for such a reception; she let loose a flow of words which must certainly have been ready in advance.

"I wouldn't talk so big, my dear girl. You're a fine one, you are! I know more about you than you think!"

With that she eyed Erica from head to toe and laughed scornfully. I felt the blood drain from my face. A few weeks before, I had got hold of a piece of good woollen material in the black market, and at Erica's insistence I had had a dressmaker cut a jacket and a pair of slacks out of it for her. I hadn't protested this strange masculine outfit, because Erica mentioned the word "warmth," and that was reason enough in those days of coal rationing. In this costume one might have taken her for a growing young man, but it would protect her from the cold.

"I'll count to thirty," said Erica. "If you aren't down the stairs by then, I'll give you a little help!"

"Erica!" I admonished her, in spite of myself.

But she ignored me; she was deathly pale now, her breath tearing through her throat, as she began counting slowly. The roles were reversed, that was clear. I realized that this same ultimatum had been offered to Erica when Ma held the upper hand—and God knows what the circumstances had been then. It was certainly not simply revenge on a normal show of parental authority.

Ma didn't make a move in the direction Erica indicated. She laughed provocatively and pulled down her girdle with the vulgar, automatic gesture of too-fat, too youthfully dressed women, and she even backed up a few steps. In doing this she held me prisoner by the hot plate, and there I stood in the steam from the boiling potatoes. My legs trembled; they could hardly hold me. I had never known that counting to thirty could last such an eternity.

"Come on, Ma! Take it easy, Erica!" I said.

Before I realized what was happening, Erica had grabbed my wrists, pulled me out of the little kitchen, and pushed me so roughly into my room that I stumbled and slid full length across the floor. She slammed my door. I remained where I was, half-stunned with shock and pain from the fall. From there I heard the wrestling in the hall, the shuffling of feet, the stumbling on the stairs, the hoarse panting of Erica, and Ma's screaming.

Then there was the voice of a neighbour downstairs, who came into the hall to ask what was the matter. On other floors, too, people were demanding an explanation. All of a sudden the house was filled with noise.

Finally Erica came upstairs and said, "That's that!" as though it had been a job settled with a simple flick of the hand.

That matter-of-fact statement was accompanied by Ma's yelling downstairs in the hall; she alternated threats and curses with explanations to the neighbours. Nobody seemed to answer her. The tenants of our building were all "on the level." I heard doors closing and knew that everybody had retired into his own apartment.

Erica stood motionless on the other side of my door; all I heard was her panting. Soon Ma had spent herself. There was the sound of her steps to the front door and a second later the door slammed.

After that Erica went to the kitchen, and I recognized the sound of a pan in the sink and the flowing of water. She was draining the potatoes. As I scrambled slowly to my feet, I realized with another shock that Erica was going downstairs. A minute later the front door closed behind her.

I visualized her standing on the doorstep, lighting a cigarette with trembling fingers. From my window I saw her cross the street hurriedly and disappear around the corner.

Chapter Eleven

A FEW days afterward, the Germans came to search the house. They arrived toward midnight and turned everything upside down. I was alone. Erica had stayed away. While I was telling them—truthfully—that she had left and that I didn't know where she was, I thought of the words of the downstairs neighbour who had come up to talk after the quarrel of that evening.

"You'd better be careful, she's a member of the Party. If she reports you...God...God!—mother and daughter!" she interrupted herself. "It's terrible these days." She was almost in tears when she left me.

After the Germans had ransacked the house, they asked me Erica's profession. I said "writer," and they finally left with a pile of notebooks in which Erica had written poetry notes years ago.

Until far into the night, I sorted out our hoard of beans and peas they had poured out on the floor. I can still feel the knobby legumes, as I picked them up one at a time and dropped each into its proper bag; I still remember the thoughts that wove and arranged themselves into new patterns.

Again it was I who stayed at home; again I had to wait for what was to happen. It seemed an eternity, but actually the fatal word reached me after just a week. Dolly came to tell me at seven o'clock in the morning that Erica was a prisoner at the City Jail.

I couldn't take it all in at once. My confusion because it was Dolly who brought the bad news...then the message

itself, which came as an anticlimax because the doorbell at
that hour had already fallen like a hammer on my heart. I
remember that I drank from the glass of ice water Dolly
handed me, and how humiliated I was, that my nerves had
given way in her presence.

"You'll most likely get an official notification," she said
right off. "I guess you can take her a change of clothes and
things like that." She stood over my chair, cool and controlled. Once more I felt insignificant and a little ridiculous
beside her. I tried to get up but my legs refused to work.

"Don't bother. Don't get up," she said. "I have to go
now. I just came to let you know. Have you got any money?
Nothing can be done without influence and money. You'll
hear from me."

She was already at the door when I called her back.
"Dolly," I said. (Even pronouncing her name was difficult
for me, for after all I had not known her, never called her
Dolly.) "Dolly, what happened? What did she do?"

"*Do?*" she laughed. "You *are* naive. You know Erica,
don't you?"

"Was she staying with you...?" I began. "How do you
know about it? When did it happen?"

"During the night. She didn't come home and I went to
inquire." Then she grinned. "Jesus, that Erica! She didn't
have a chance in the world, and yet...She knew about the
searching of the house from one of your neighbours who is
in the movement. She was betrayed, of course, and you can
imagine who it was. I had forbidden her..."

She was silent, and looked searchingly at me for a
moment. Then her eyes grew hard again, as cold and
unfeeling as they had been that time in her studio.

"If you weren't such a nincompoop! What she sees in
you, God knows. Neither fish nor fowl. Why don't you let

her go? What do you get out of it? Well, it's none of my business. The important thing is to get her out. You'll hear from me."

But it was hopeless. I tried everything: the impossible, the lowest things I could think of. Dolly was my accomplice, my support and refuge. Through her, I got into contact with the underground movement. I was referred to a lawyer in The Hague who had connections, but he asked eight thousand guilders and I didn't have that, and I couldn't get it together with all the help in the world—though I went to every extreme to get it. I even went to beg from Pa. He swore he didn't have it but I saw the turmoil inside him.

"That's only to be expected," Dolly said when I told her of his refusal later. "He needed it for himself, for his own flight. He got the hell out."

How did she know that, I wondered.

"I went myself after you'd failed. I'm better suited for jobs like that than you are. But he had flown the coop."

I braced myself. "Ma," I said. "Blackmail."

There was that word again, so familiar now, so easy to say after the days of thinking, of going over and over the dialogue with Ma.

Dolly shrugged. "Have you got any proof? Not a chance in the world, darling!"

Still I tried, and I shall never forget the torture of that enterprise.

Ma was on her high horse. "She's excellently treated there. It will do her good, teach her a lesson. She doesn't need anything. Besides, I send her a package every week—anonymous, of course. Before you know it she'll be here with you again. Don't worry. You'll see that the Germans aren't as black as they are painted."

I saved my trump card for last. But Ma broke in on me after a few words; that was enough. She knew what I was driving at.

"See if you can prove it. And I'd be careful if I were you. Before you know it, you'll be behind bars yourself. And I'll tell you another thing, young lady. Even if they believed it, even if you could prove it, they wouldn't think any less of me. Pa was a Jew—don't forget that! One Jew was enough for me! And now you'd better go home. Your dear friend will be home in a few weeks. Then you two can..."

I didn't let her finish, for if she had completed that sentence I would have attacked her and ruined my last chances.

"But after all, she is your child, Ma!" I implored, though the words almost choked me.

"Yes—and a lot of pleasure I got from her! Small thanks for my trouble. All my sacrifices for nothing. All my life I've worked for her...the best education...the finest schools..."

"Erica realizes that very well, Ma. She often talks about it." I went on with my betrayal, for that was what it was. Erica must never know about this visit. My lying words didn't fail to impress Ma. She grew visibly mellower, and switched to the role of the misunderstood but resigned mother.

"You see, Bea, you are still young; you can't really understand it, child, but no sacrifice is too much for a mother to make. But then, if it is all wasted, well...let me be honest with you. If a child then grows up to be abnormal.... And God knows how she got to be that way; she certainly didn't get it from my side of the family!" A coquettish smile passed across her face. "Well, anyway...you understand me. No gratitude, no love, ever." Sentimental tears welled in her eyes.

"But you can't let your own child sit in prison! After all, you do have influence and a position in the Party."

"Everything will be all right," Ma said quickly. "Don't get so upset."

Later at Dolly's I cried, and for the first time in all those weeks she gave me her sympathy.

"Oh, you little fool! What a mess! And what a stupid bitch that woman is. She really thinks they will stand Erica in a corner with a dunce cap on for a little while and then let her go!"

Yes, Dolly and I were accomplices—almost friends. I learned to appreciate her, and she no longer showed contempt for me.

The weeks drew on into months. Life became more difficult daily, but the hardships hardly touched me. I waited; I could do no more. Sometimes I went to Dolly's, and we would sit in almost complete silence by her little wood-stove, in the room that used to belong to Erica.

In February there was a kind of trial, at which I saw Erica once more. She smiled at us, at Dolly and me. Soon afterward she was sent to the concentration camp at Vught, and in April I received notice of her death.

It said "Pneumonia" on the card I took from the mailbox.

Afterword

DOLA DE JONG'S *The Tree and the Vine* was first published in the Netherlands in 1955 and appeared in translation in Great Britain in 1961 and the United States in 1963. Unfortunately, the English translation had little impact in its day, perhaps because it failed to get the reviews it deserved. *The Statesman and Nation* reviewer (May 12, 1961), for example, unable to appreciate the book's subtleties and larger meanings, described its content in silly, cliché terms that were characteristic of cover copy for the lesbian pulps of the era: "exotic vices," "[a] harrowing account of the disintegration of a character under the impact of compulsive sin," "the world of the sexual pervert." Indeed, there are elements in *The Tree and the Vine* that capture the flavor of the 1950s lesbian pulps, but it took a reviewer as astute as V. S. Naipaul, writing for *The Listener* (June 16, 1961), to see its "delicacy" and its "touching" quality. Contemporary readers will be able to appreciate the ways in which the novel transcends the genre of the pulps in its complex presentation of characters whose quiet and not-so-quiet tragedies of self-deception and self-destruction play themselves out against the backdrop of the Netherlands in the late 1930s, on the eve of the Nazi invasion.

Beatrice, de Jong's first person narrator, is a psychological study of the repressed lesbian who denies her desires even as she obsessively pursues them. Bea is the classic unreliable narrator, and as such she presents a challenge to the reader. The author beckons us to see around and between and beneath Bea's words, intending that we understand

Bea's lesbianism long before she has any notion about what is transpiring within herself. For instance, though Bea refuses self-knowledge, the reader is meant to interpret the apparent significance of her past sexual history—those few, short, violent sexual relationships with men that only led her to depression. De Jong wishes us also to be aware, as Bea is not, of the significance of her immediate attraction to Erica whose boyish garb and boy's haircut are semiotic for "the lesbian." Despite the willful density of the unreliable narrator, we must know the meaning of her fascination with Erica's smells, that sexy mixture of cigarette smoke and lavender soap. (And how can we miss the significance of "lavender" in lesbian iconography?)

De Jong also permits us to understand much more than Bea is willing to acknowledge about her attitude towards Erica's other associates. "What did Erica look for in a girlfriend?" the author lets Bea naively wonder. "Why did she want to live with me if her preference was so clearly for loud, vulgar, superficial creatures such as Judy and Dolly?" Her jealousy, expressed in unconvincing tones of superiority, is transparent. Her use of the ambiguous term "girlfriend" is patently disingenuous—as is her refusal to acknowledge that she desires to assume the role of Erica's femme when she irons her clothes: She claims that her purpose in taking care of Erica's needs in that way is that she wants to keep her from looking like "an ill-groomed boy," but de Jong lets us see through that pretense as Bea repeatedly betrays her feelings while denying them. When Bea finally must admit to herself her realization that Erica is a lesbian she proclaims that there is a difference between them, and she declares they must each go their own way. But we know long before she does that she will be compelled to pursue her unutterable and ineluctable attraction to Erica. The narrator's lack of self-knowledge forces the reader into the interesting role of analyst.

And there is much for an analyst to work with in this little tale. De Jong depicts the pain of sexual obsession, which is rendered even more painful by Bea's denial of the possibility of its existence: How can she be obsessed with lesbian desire when she is not a lesbian? Yet she cannot stay away from Erica: Bea avows they must not live together; she tells herself that Erica would only lead her to a "strange existence" that was not her own; she does everything she can to separate herself from this fatal woman. And then she finds herself haunting the vicinity of the newspaper building where Erica works, daring—or beseeching—fate to bring them together again. Yet even the evidence of her own actions is not enough to force Bea to "admit it," as Erica demands of her—to acknowledge both that she is a lesbian and that she is in love. Bea must swallow three bromide tablets in order to write Erica, to say that she, Bea, "belonged to another world than hers." But she never sends the letter. The next morning she lets its pages fly in pieces from the train window. Though she cannot articulate the change in herself, we know that her resolve has broken down entirely.

Bea's difficulty in admission is not due simply to a remarkable dishonesty or density. To have acknowledged one's lesbian identity in the 1930s, in this "world of the sexual pervert," "compulsive sin," and "exotic vices," would have been to assume an overwhelming and impossible burden for so timid a person as Bea is, a "Miss Milquetoast," as Erica calls her. But although Bea cannot call herself a lesbian, her passion finally leads her to total commitment to Erica. What is the meaning of that commitment? An earlier era might have seen it as an expression of "romantic friendship" and the sexual implications of Bea's feelings might conceivably have been denied. But Bea lives in a Freudian era, in which the luxury of such denial is no longer possible. As disturbing as it may be to her, ultimately she cannot escape understanding what she has such difficulty admitting: that she desires Erica.

Though she is too frightened to pursue direct experience, her desire expresses itself for a period in a timid voyeurism: She is relieved to be able to experience a lesbian "union" vicariously at least, whenever Inge spends the night with Erica in the apartment that Bea and Erica share: "I lived for those evenings," Bea manages to articulate. Her timid, vicarious pleasure is as pathetic as her earlier denial was. But before the novel is over she is able to express her desire more nobly and bravely, through her loving and unflagging attempts, doomed to failure by Erica's self-destructiveness, to rescue Erica, a Bastard-Jew I, according to Nazi classification, from what will be inevitable when the Nazis invade.

Despite Bea's final heroic efforts on Erica's behalf, it is only in retrospect that she can fully acknowledge what Erica really meant to her. In America during the 1950s, looking back on her experience of the Netherlands in the 1930s, she recognizes that Erica was her "main event," the only important event of her life. While she has continued to have brief heterosexual affairs, she says, "men are like shadows in the background of my life." It is Erica who occupied the spotlight, who "played the leading role." Long after Erica's death, Bea is tormented by what she finally considers her inappropriate self-control which forbade the fulfillment of her longings: She asks herself now, "Why...had [I] put these restrictions on our relationship[?]" Now she is eaten up by regret for what she has missed and the pathetic realization that "After all, it can never be amended, never lived again."

The poignancy of the situation, as Bea ultimately sees it and as de Jong wishes the reader to see it, derives from the sad fact that Bea refused to permit herself to live fully with the only person who created full desire in her.

De Jong had several models for her characters, both in literature of the 1930s and in the post-World War II pulps. Perhaps the most obvious model for Erica was Robin Vote, the devastatingly alluring and neurotic androgyne in Djuna Barnes's 1937 novel, *Nightwood*. Like beautiful Robin in her "boy's pants," the fascination of Erica in this pre-unisex era lies in her boy-girl quality. Bea has "never seen a woman who could do carpentry as well as she"; Bea is intrigued by Erica's "shiny boy's haircut and her sloppy boy's shirts and her sock-clad legs." Like Robin, Erica wanders at night in mysterious places, drinks herself sick, sleeps around indiscriminately. And like Barnes's Nora, whose love is manifested in her futile attempts to rescue Robin from herself, Bea attempts to rescue her beloved androgyne from her self-destructive drives, cleaning up after Erica, sacrificing and demeaning herself, always to no avail.

Such depictions of painful and futile relationships between women became the stuff of the lesbian pulp novels that were sold from drugstore bookracks all over America after the war. Although the quality and seriousness of de Jong's book far transcend those pulps, there is much that is familiar here and can be explained as a function of the times in which de Jong was writing. Lesbian novels of the 1950s almost invariably betray the influence of their era: Censorship laws, the tyranny of conventional morality, and the heterocentric convictions of the Freudians (who were the high priests of the 1950s) all colluded to make the notion of a "well-adjusted lesbian" oxymoronic. Relations

between women in literature were invariably doomed to
failure—not only for the interesting reasons of self-denial
and cowardice that Beatrice reveals, but also frequently
because lesbians just can't seem to "get along" or they are
innately capricious or nasty. Women in "Erica's situation"—
that is, lesbians—as even Bea observes from her still-safe
perch, "always swing to extremes in love as well as in animosity." Bea's point is illustrated when Erica and Judy are
seen at one moment to "hit and scratch" and at the next to
be "closely entwined." Dolly (Erica's lover who follows
promiscuously close on the heels of Judy) attacks Erica
repeatedly, throws her down the stairs, and is declared by
Erica to be "sadistic by nature." The lesbian twilight world,
even in de Jong's novel, is depicted as being not a very safe
or pretty place.

Self-hatred, pain, and defiant pride in one's "abnormality" are also stock for the genre of the pulps of pre-lesbian
feminism, and we see the influence of those mid-century
concepts in *The Tree and the Vine*, too. Erica declares her
lesbianism to Bea in a melodramatic scene: "'That's the way
I am!' she shouted at me then. 'That's how I am.' Her face,
wet with tears and distorted in an expression of pain and triumph at the same time..." Erica calls her lesbian state "being
wrong," and she comes to accept it by "resign[ing] herself."

"Abnormality" such as Erica's was also invariably traced
to a "cause" in lesbian novels of the era: There must be an
etiology that "explains" the "abnormality." Here, too, de
Jong was constrained by the demands of the era in which
she was writing. In Erica's case one does not have far to look
for the "cause" of her lesbianism: Her childhood predetermined what she has become. Her mother, who was sicken-
ingly vain in her femininity as well as domineering and
unloving, not only was without mothering skills but also

presented a role model to be avoided for a serious young girl seeking who to be as a woman. In the views of the 1950s, it is no wonder that Erica needs to find satisfaction with a female since she got none from her mother in childhood; it is no wonder that she is an androgyne since her mother did not show her how to be a plausible woman. Moreover, her father was absent so she could not form early positive relations with males, de Jong implies. And before her father deserted them, he and her mother constantly fought. Erica saw no examples of a happy heterosexual relationship. To clinch it all, de Jong suggests that, when Erica was sixteen she was "locked up" in the "'abnormal' atmosphere of the convent," where, of course, her young sexual longings were perverted in the direction of lesbianism. The formula will be entirely familiar to students of the pulps and of the 1950s Freudians. Even Bea's repressed desires are given a psychological explanation: When she was a child her mother died giving birth to a male infant. As simplistic as such "etiologies" may appear in a postmodernist era, we must remember that it was virtually impossible to write a novel about lesbianism in the 1950s without devoting space to the "cause" of the "condition."

The inevitability of the discovery of the "true self" that must come out, another cliché of the pulps (and very different from our postmodernist notions about the flexibility and fluidity of sexuality), is also insisted upon in this novel. Though Erica's lesbianism has been "predetermined for her," as Bea says, by her childhood, she is naive about her proclivities at the start, if we can believe her account to Bea. Her relationship with Wies, she claims, was "fairly innocent, sexually speaking," though they slept in the same bed. "At that time I wasn't doing that sort of thing yet." But others, more knowledgable about "that sort of thing," know what

she "really" is. Her employer, Van der Lelie, Erica recalls to
Bea, "had seen through me before I had even seen through
myself." He accused her of lesbian interests, though she was
herself unconscious of them. That accusation served as a
revelation to her. In her unconscious lesbianism she was like
a lion cub, oblivious to her big paws which everyone else can
see and which she must inevitably grow into; and also like
the lion, once she assumes her true lesbian state, she is fero-
cious and lethal, "a dangerous girl," Bas tells her when he
warns her away from Bea.

Finally, the melodrama that overtakes *The Tree and the
Vine* at midpoint is also characteristic of lesbian novels of its
era. Before the concept of love between women is rescued
in this novel by Bea's nobility of devotion, it is seen to lead
to a hopelessness that brings misery; it is connected to sor-
did images such as Erica sleeping off a drunk in the flat she
shares with her lover, Dolly, her hat and coat in vomit on the
floor, Dolly refusing to help her because she believes
"tomorrow it would be the same thing again." Erica's self-
destructive impulse, which perhaps causes her to spend the
money Judy sent so that she could rescue herself, is born of
her self-hatred that—in good pulp fashion—has its genesis
in her lesbianism.

If *The Tree and the Vine* belonged simply to the genre of
the lesbian pulps the novel would have little but historical
interest for today's reader. De Jong manages, however, to
go far beyond that black-and-white genre in this shaded,
nuanced tale of wasted life and missed lives. Though the
reader is sometimes frustrated in attempting to see Erica
fully, what we glimpse leads to fascinating and provocative
questions: Why does she play a game of flirtation and
seduction with a frightened little mouse such as Bea? Or is

she playing a game? Is the game only Bea's in her refusal to admit what she knows all too well? If Erica is so powerful as to be as coolly in control of Bea, as Bea sometimes seems to want us to believe, why does Erica appear to be so manipulated by her other lovers?—by Judy who plays the lesbian with her "only for a thrill," by Dolly who speaks of her "in a tone one might apply to a sick dog," by Inge at whose feet she sits and who deceives her by fleeing the country without warning? Is Erica a carnivorous flower, as Bea usually seems to suggest she is? Or is she the pathetic victim of other, stronger women?

Other interesting questions abound. Why is Erica's behavior so self-destructive? Why does she return to Dolly after Dolly attacks her three times and throws her down the stairs? Does she repeatedly drink herself sick because she is devastated by the discovery that she is a lesbian and a Jew in a homophobic, antisemitic era—or is it because of her miserable childhood, or does she simply enjoy it? Does she neglect to follow through on her investigation about whether or not her putative Polish father was really Jewish because she is too busy with decadent pleasures, or because she has a death wish, or because she is disgusted by the absurdity of Hitler's racial theories and refuses to be complicitous in his repulsive racial game? Does she squander her escape money and neglect to utilize what is left of her legacy in order to leave Nazi Europe because she is so involved with Inge—or is it because she cannot believe, until it is too late, that she is in danger? Is she like Bea's boss, who feels himself to be more Dutch than Jewish and is thus puzzled by the notion that one must "escape" from the Netherlands—or is it that she makes no move to escape because she hates herself? Is she really purposely self-destructive, or simply immature or naive? She is, after all, terribly young when Bea first meets her, barely out of childhood.

Bea warns us at the beginning of the novel that while she had hoped repeatedly to have some final insight into Erica, the mystery of her beloved eluded her to the very end. She was never able to discover whether what she had been observing was "a growing tree" or "a lifeless trunk, its own greenery stifled by the vines that grew around it." That mystery eludes us, too. But we are able to see enough, as subtle as de Jong's touch often is, to understand what would appeal to Bea, why she obsessed about achieving her "insight" into this rakish young *voyoue* who is her diametrical opposite—who, when they hardly know each other, leans against Bea sleepily, telling her she is a "sweet little bitch" and kissing her on the neck, who sings vulgar Dutch ditties but is ultimately transformed into a serious underground resistance fighter. The book is sexually charged through these mysterious, tantalizing, contradictory glimpses of the object of Bea's fascination.

Though to the end we as well as Bea know little about who Erica really is, we learn a good deal about who Bea really is. While for Bea it is Erica who is the only focus of attention, for the reader, as we watch the watcher watch, it is Bea in her lack of self-knowledge, her tragic self-denials, her movement from timidity to noble expansiveness, who is the most interesting character. The Bea who appears early in the novel is not very likable or alluring. She reveals herself to be hypocritical, narrow, and judgmental. She proclaims that she maintains a friendship with Wies, whom she dislikes, because she is unwilling to offend people, though she disdains what she characterizes as Wies's "thickness of skin" and penchant to spread out and tighten a net of female solidarity with all women that she meets. Bea, in contrast to Wies, is a loner, reluctant to reveal who she is to others almost as much as she hides from herself. Unlike Wies, Bea feels solidarity with no one when we first meet her; she belongs to nothing; she views life only from the periphery. Before the novel is over she will learn to become engaged in life.

Bea's initial hypocrisy is manifested further in her tight-lipped, puritanical attitude toward the sensual indulgences that money can buy. She only perfunctorily resists the gifts, the unaccustomed luxuriousness of restaurants and plays and concerts, that Erica bestows on her with the legacy from the "childless uncle." Rather than admitting her pleasure in these treats, she tells herself she abhors Erica's mad haste to be spendthrift and she is anxious for the money and the indulgences to come to an end: "I could not bear the feverish atmosphere, the artificial gaiety," she declares, missing the point that one of Erica's many attractions for her has to do with the fact that Erica is compulsively spendthrift about life.

When Bea tells her tale, she is looking back from the perspective of 1953 on the person she was in the late 1930s. Experience has broadened her perspective, as her retrospective narrative voice occasionally hints. The extent to which she has changed in the present of 1953 is suggested in part through her reflections on the bohemian quarters where Erica lived with Dolly. Bea tells us that in the 1930s, on seeing their building, it seemed to her to be one of those places "which should have been declared uninhabitable," a house that attracted those who may have considered themselves "artistically inclined" but in their aspirations were merely pretentious. "Real, hard-working artists," she believed in the 1930s (characterizing her past reflections in her present voice as a "pedantry" that supported her unwarranted self-confidence), "would live in solid buildings where work can go on without the daily intrusion of wear and decay." Her present voice also portrays her as critical of her earlier narrow and glib judgments about various arts: "I did not know anything about dancers," she now reflects, "and I must confess that at the time I looked down on them. Or, more accurately, I was suspicious of anyone whose ambition was to jump around on a stage and twist her body into all sorts of contortions." It is the mystifying and inconclusive experience with Erica that finally gives her a blessed humility and teaches her not to be so hurried in her pronouncements, so quick to rush to judgment.

Before her metamorphosis, Bea is unlovely in this quickness to judge and her general disagreeableness. To the young Bea nothing passes without her pat pronouncement and her sniff of superiority. But the novel is largely about who she will become, and those changes begin even at the opening of the book, when she is immediately attracted to Erica and confused by that attraction because she never liked such "types" before. Bea remembers their first encounter: "She was dressed more or less like a member of the Socialist Youth Organization—a particular type with which I had never felt at ease. We had a few girls like that working at the office and I always kept away from them." She has shielded herself from any human experience that discomfited her, and now she has much to learn about the permeability of shields as well the problem with snap and superficial judgements. Her learning will not be easy. We can predict from the outset that the fates, with their quirky predilection for irony, have in store for her lessons to be learned by raw suffering.

Indeed, Bea tells us early in the novel how different she is now from the person she was when the story began: She declares that Erica "changed the course of my life." It is the story of that change that gives *The Tree and the Vine* its force.

There is not much to like or empathize with in the Bea of 1938, but in the course of her development she wins the reader's pity for what she misses and finally the reader's admiration for what she achieves—her ability to go outside of herself, to devote herself selflessly.

The novel's impact is heightened by the historical tensions de Jong presents. Her characters are not only struggling with their own repressions and neuroses and conflicted personalities. They are ultimately under the control of a tremendous external force: As it becomes clear that the Nazis will take over the Netherlands and that Erica will be in great danger because she is considered a Jew, the tragedy of the timid lover and the doomed beloved takes on far greater proportions. The characters are defeated not only by "what is false within," as George Meredith explained doomed love relationships, but also by the impersonal, implacable, and finally victorious enemy. If it had not been for the Nazi invasion...if Bea had had more time to grow out of her timidity...if Erica had not been killed...

It is at the point in the novel when the Nazi occupation becomes inevitable that the characters take on nuances that give the book its tragic and most interesting dimension. Because of Bea's obsession with Erica she has been unable to perceive early what the Nazis have in store for the Netherlands. Bea tells us that during the first year of her obsession the world had drifted irrevocably to the edge of the precipice, but she remained unmoved by the shocking events in Spain, Austria, Germany, and Asia. Her metaphor suggests the mindlessness and oblivion of her obsession: She was blind to Hitler's threat because "I had moved like a riding horse in training; blinders prevented me from seeing anything but Erica, who was trotting in front of me, whom I could not, and was not allowed to, overtake." However, the growing fascist threat finally impinges itself on her consciousness. It is not clear that she understands that homosexuals were sent to death camps under Hitler's regime. But she does understand the danger all European Jews were in. Believing that Erica is Jewish, Bea awakens to the problems of her Jewish boss, who must escape from the Netherlands though he feels like a deserter because he has always considered himself more Dutch than Jewish. He is ashamed to be leaving his country and feels guilty towards other Jews who do not have the money to escape as he does. Slowly Bea begins to realize how dire are the circumstances.

Once Bea understands the situation she becomes alarmed that Erica does not. De Jong reveals that for an individual like Erica, the Nazis' antisemitic concepts were entirely confusing. If her mother's Jewish husband is really her father—or if the Polish violinist whom she is now told was her father is Jewish—then she is Jewish under Hitler's racial theories. And yet she has never considered herself a Jew. How can she take those theories seriously when they have nothing to do with her self-conception? "Ridiculous!" she exclaims. "Now I am suddenly a Jewess." Yet whether she sees it as ridiculous or not, as Bea points out, her fate in the hands of the Nazis "would be little different from that of the 'real' Jews."

How hard it must have been to make sense of such a situation: Though Erica has had no Jewish religious or cultural upbringing and no reason to consider herself Jewish, she is considered a Jew by others, and if she wishes to survive she must acknowledge that she is in danger as a Jew. "America, America, here I come," she proclaims, though Bea is not convinced that Erica really sees the danger and speculates that Erica considers leaving Europe only "because her personal difficulties [in love relationships] had forced her to seek a change." However, Erica's astonishment and ambivalence are only temporary. She soon understands that being Jewish under Hitler's regime is no more a "choice" than being lesbian has been for her. But de Jong implies that though an individual cannot chose to accept or reject the states of Jewishness or lesbianism which heredity, environment, or political circumstances impose on her, she can determine what she will do within them. Erica reacts to her lesbian state by dissipation; she finally reacts to her Jewish state by heroic activism. She is thus not only redeemed as a moral being but is also made even more romantic and tragic in Bea's eyes. The fact of the Nazi invasion tests and alters both Erica and Bea.

When the Nazis occupy the Netherlands, Bea's early oblivion is entirely eradicated because Erica is threatened. At that point—when she understands that the person she loves may be doomed—she can finally admit her love to herself: Bea asks to see Erica so that she can remind her of the danger she is in as a presumed Jew. As she concludes her panicked speech, she realizes that Erica "knew at last what went on inside me. And then I knew myself, too." This mutual acknowledgment leads to Bea's irrevocable commitment to Erica, which they also both now understand. From this point on Bea can no longer turn back. Erica puts her arms around her, pressing Bea tightly to her, and Bea does not resist. We are not privy to what it is Erica whispers in Bea's ear, but de Jong's provocative lines confirm its significance: "Those few words she never spoke again; it was not necessary. We both knew they were irrevocable, and for ever we accepted them, each in her own way."

While the Nazi Occupation puts an end to any possibility of a fulfilled relationship between Bea and Erica—and, indeed, to Erica herself—it is the external threat occasioned by the Occupation that gives both Bea and Erica reason and spur to develop their capacities for noble, self-transcending behavior. It is the war that defeats them; but it is also the war that saves them—that causes them to become serious human beings. Erica's new-found seriousness as a resistance worker is the most obvious. But de Jong also suggests Bea's transformation. She is no longer ironing Erica's clothes under the pretense that Erica would otherwise look like an ill-groomed boy. Now her occupations in serving Erica are significant and heroic. There is no longer room for self-deception. Nothing matters to her now outside of helping the threatened beloved.

Her desperation is poignant: Bea tries to get the truth about Erica's birth from her mother. She rushes to the American consulate and the shipping company in Erica's service. She pretends to have a nervous breakdown in order to try to save Erica from being killed in the underground movement. She pawns her grandmother's jewelry to buy a forged identity card for Erica. She desperately tries to raise eight thousand guilders for the lawyer's fee in the hope that the lawyer will be able to help get Erica released from prison. Obviously many of her actions on Erica's behalf could have placed her in personal danger, but she is not mindful of those risks. Bea is quite transformed from her earlier role as a "Miss Milquetoast." And though she may have an ulterior motive for her heroism in her desire, her actions are nevertheless heroic.

Though Bea later blames herself for not having dared to fulfill her desire for Erica in those months when Erica was entirely dependent on her, her selfless service is perhaps all the more ennobled because she refrains from claiming a fleshly reward. At the start of the novel Bea thinks much too highly of herself, while the reader sees her pettiness. At the conclusion, after her transformation, we see that she does not think highly enough of herself. She does not credit herself enough for fine behavior, but we must credit her.

Just as Bea's heroism develops along lines not inconsistent with her character and her earlier obsessive focus on Erica, so does Erica evolve into her heroism in ways characteristic of her. Throughout the novel Erica had been reckless in pursuit of pleasure and self-punishment. In the last chapters of the novel she becomes reckless for a noble cause—resistance to the Nazis. Erica is involved in the early stages of sabotage against the Nazi occupation to such an extent that even she must wonder at the daring of her actions. Bea observes that Erica's work as a resistance fighter puts her in even greater danger than her uncertain origin, but she also understands that Erica's heroic actions are a manifestation of who she is, expressed in terms the situation now demands of her. The appeal to Erica of sabotage against the Nazis stems not only from the fact that "it suited her character perfectly to be doing illegal things," as Bea observes at one point, but also from the fact, as Bea also realizes, that "she could not compromise and make the best of it; she couldn't stay out of the line of fire like the mass of the population." The Nazi horror, ironically, creates the opportunity for Erica to transform her penchant for self-indulgent and destructive recklessness into bravery. De Jong's setting of the novel on the eve of and in the course of the Nazi Occupation thus works brilliantly to develop dimension in the characters and power in their story.

Lillian Faderman
Fresno, California

About the Author

THERE is much in this haunting little book that suggests Dola de Jong's firsthand experiences. She was born in the Netherlands in 1911. Like Erica, she became a journalist when very young, after graduating from high school. Like Dolly, she later became a professional dancer and was a member of the Royal Dutch Ballet for eight years. In the late 1930s, disturbed by Hitler's fascism and antisemitism, she played the role of Bea with her family, trying to convince them to leave the Netherlands. They, however, were "Ericas" and remained. Her father, stepmother, and a brother were murdered by the Nazis. Another brother was imprisoned in the Netherlands and survived the war.

De Jong fled from the Netherlands to Morocco in 1940. In 1941, she emigrated to the United States, like Bea, and became a citizen in 1947. The urgencies and life-threatening situations created by the Second World War also play a large part in an earlier novel by de Jong, *The Field*, about European Jewish children fleeing the Nazi holocaust, who are transplanted to a farm near Tangier. *The Field* won the National Prize for Literature in the Netherlands in 1947 and was later published in the United States by Scribner.

Dola de Jong's first book, written in Dutch, appeared in 1936, when she was twenty-five years old. Throughout the 1930s de Jong wrote and published books in Dutch for young adults. In 1941 she became a foreign correspondent and also soon began writing and publishing books in English as well as Dutch. In 1960 she was elected to membership in the Dutch Academy of Letters. De Jong also developed a successful career as a mystery writer with award-winning novels such as *The House on Charlton Street* (1962) and *The Whirligig of Time* (1964). She has published sixteen books of her own writing and has edited an anthology of American short stories for Dutch readers. Dola de Jong currently lives in New York.

L. F.